THE
STORM

THE STORM

THOMAS CLARK

LUMINARE PRESS

WWW.LUMINAREPRESS.COM

Printed in the United States of America

Cover Design: Clark Concepts, LLC

Luminare Press
442 Charnelton St.
Eugene, OR 97401
www.luminarepress.com

LCCN: 2019910807
ISBN: 978-1-64388-183-6

For
Brian, Brendon, & Robin

CHAPTER ONE

Before starting the long trip, the two guards transporting him to Tennessee had made sure the chain connecting Sonny's ankle and wrist restraints was a foot too short. "A little going-away present for you, Masters," was the way the heavy one in the driver's seat had put it, shoving him into the back seat of the prison van. It was an old trick used when transporting inmates the guards would have given a month's pay to club to death, a status Sonny Masters had achieved within days of his arrival at the Western Maryland Correctional Center. Without the freedom to sit up straight, Sonny's back was killing him before they had traveled fifty miles, a fact he would not have shared with the two pricks in the front seat for a million dollars.

Somewhere in southern Virginia they turned off the main highway to look for a barbecue place the driver had heard about from his brother-in-law. A clutter of gasoline stations with signs mounted atop sky-scraping poles hugged the exit ramps but, beyond these, they found nothing but a two-lane road weaving an endless path through planted fields and pinewoods.

"You sure this is the right way?"

"Exit 217, westbound. That's what he wrote down."

At the bottom of a steep hill, they crossed a wide creek and slowed in front of a small restaurant squeezed between the creek and a white church wrapped in a blanket of vines. Red neon tubing in the window flashed the words *Bar-B-Q* at the lone pickup truck in the gravel parking lot.

"That ain't it. He said it had a pig on the roof."

The road climbed away from the creek and wound through contoured fields of young corn.

"We must have passed it," the guard in the passenger seat said as thick woods took the place of open fields.

"He said it was a ways."

"Comfortable back there, Masters?" the guard in the passenger seat turned to ask for the twentieth time, a witticism that never failed to make the driver laugh like it was the funniest thing he had ever heard.

The storm that had formed inside Sonny when he was a boy raged dangerously. He wanted to kill them; whatever it took, he wanted to kill them both, a couple of punks who would not have had the guts to look him in the eye if he weren't chained like an animal. Blood pulsed wildly behind his eyes as his muscular arms tightened and his big hands rolled into fists as hard as hammers.

"How about that chain? Long enough for you?" The driver laughed like an idiot again.

Sonny held his tongue. He closed his eyes, breathed deeply, and reminded himself that the only thing that mattered was for him to stay cool and stick to his plan.

As they rounded a long bend in the road the trees gave way to an overgrown hillside cemetery whose perimeter was defined by the remains of an ancient metal fence. The driver pulled onto the narrow shoulder and unfolded a hand-drawn map. "I wonder if we passed it," he said, squinting at the penciled lines and markings before handing it to his partner.

Above the cemetery, the ruins of a house trailer squatted in a nest of junk like a giant roosting hen. Wisps of white smoke twisted from a stovepipe chimney and vanished in the harsh summer light. As Sonny watched, the trailer's slatted glass door swung open and a shirtless boy came outside, threw an empty bottle into the sea of waist-high weeds, and sat down on the pile of concrete blocks forming a precarious set of steps. For a few seconds he stared down the hill at the prison van, then stretched his thin young body and looked away.

"Maybe it was that first place."

"He said it had a pig on the roof."

"Well, shit, we can't drive around all day."

Sonny kept his eyes on the boy as the van pulled back onto the road and continued up the hill. He watched him until the weed-covered field gave way to another grove of pine trees, erasing the boy and his hopeless world from

3

view. Sonny raised his knees slowly, creating just enough slack in the chain to allow him to ease his head back and think. He wondered if the boy had any half-decent clothes to wear to school, clothes good enough to keep him from being the laughingstock of the playground. He wondered if the boy knew what it was like to be led to a basket of used clothes in the principal's office and ordered to find some shirts and pants and a pair of shoes his size. Had he grown strong enough and smart enough to realize that the only way to stop the laughter and cruel words was by beating the living shit out of his biggest and loudest tormentor? Beat his fucking brains out in front of the rest of them so that they all understood. Sonny closed his eyes and waited for his heart to slow. It had been the same way when he got to prison. He had been tested, he had been pushed, and it had been made very clear to him that there was a pecking order for everything and, as the new boy—the name they called him until they learned the hard way not to—he was expected to speak when spoken to and stay out of the way of the big dogs. Sonny smiled, thinking about those assholes.

"I'll be goddamned!"

"I told you, smart-ass. Is that a pig on the roof or not?"

The two guards shared high fives as they pulled off the road.

"I'll stay here and watch him," the one in the passenger seat announced, gesturing with his thumb toward the back seat. "Get me a pulled pork with coleslaw, fries, and a big Coke."

4

"Should we get him anything?" the driver asked. "Krebs gave me meal money for all three of us."

"Fuck him. We'll use his for a couple of beers after we drop him off."

Sonny cursed silently as the shackles dug into his wrists. He wasn't going to say anything and he wasn't going to do anything. It was going to take time to change his reputation but it was the only way. He was going to be a model prisoner at the new place. No more fighting, no more mouthing off at guards. The people in Tennessee were going to think they had been sent the wrong person.

"What do you think, Masters, is the Bull going to be top dog again now that you're gone?"

He was talking about an inmate they called the Baltimore Bull who had ruled the prison in Maryland until Sonny got there. The Bull's seat in the dining hall was back in a corner where he could watch everything that went on, surrounded by a circle of lapdogs who delivered messages for him, laughed at his crude jokes, and eagerly offered him their coffee or slice of pie if he so much as glanced at it. On Sonny's first day, as though it were a part of the official prison orientation, he was informed by his nervous cellmate that the Bull did not allow anyone except those in his circle of flunkies to make eye contact with him. It was an offense that had recently cost another new inmate most of his teeth. That day at lunch, Sonny made eye contact. The Bull stared back in disbelief and literally came out of his chair when Sonny winked at him.

Sonny loved to think about it. He had fought bigger

men; he had fought football players and ex-boxers and black belts who came at him with karate moves accented with a bunch of stupid grunts. The Bull never knew what hit him. The beating Sonny put on the man cost him a month in solitary, but it had cost the Bull his reputation. As the months dragged by there had been others, mostly new guys looking to make their own reputation. Sonny made sure none of them ever tried twice.

The two guards ate their barbeque and drank their Cokes in front of him, the one in the passenger's seat turning from time to time to squeeze a French fry through the heavy steel screen in front of Sonny. "Want another one, huh? Want another one?" Sonny said nothing.

The driver belched, rolled the greasy wrapper and sauce-stained napkins into a tight ball, and stuffed them into his empty Coke cup. "Goddamn good barbecue; told you it would be."

"Not half bad," his partner agreed. "You ready to roll?"

"Not yet. Got to piss."

Sonny had to piss, too, and he said so, the first words he had uttered on the entire trip. The guards looked at each other.

"Let him piss in his pants," the one in the passenger seat said.

The driver laughed nervously. "We can't do that. The people down in Tennessee might report it to Lieutenant Krebs."

He started the SUV and followed a driveway to the rear of the restaurant. There, between a dumpster and an abandoned pickup truck, the two men with un-holstered handguns laughed their asses off watching Sonny struggle against his chains to pull out his dick and take a leak.

"Don't get any on that nice yellow jumpsuit," one of them bellowed, slapping his partner on the shoulder. "Watch out for your shoes!"

Sonny closed his eyes and concentrated on his plan. No more trouble. No more fighting. No more mouthing off at guards. He had thought it all through the last time he was in solitary. So what if he had beaten the living shit out of any inmate who had thought they could push him around? So what if he had refused to take any shit off the guards, no matter how many times they dragged him out of sight and did things every last one of them would later swear had never happened? When his knuckles healed and the welts on his back and legs faded he was still in prison, walls and bars and razor wire separating him from a world where the three people in the crosshairs of his hatred basked in the mistaken belief that they had seen the last of Sonny Masters.

The only thing that mattered was escaping. All the fighting he had done since they slammed the prison doors behind him had been stupid. All it had done was buy him increasingly long stints in solitary and, finally, this transfer. His head was now screwed on straight. No matter how much shit he had to take from anyone, he was not going to do one thing that kept him from inching closer to his freedom. He no longer gave a damn about people like the Bull or the two punk guards in the front seat. At the new place he was going to be Model Prisoner Number One. It might take a while, but eventually they were going to get tired of watching him like a hawk and wonder what the people up in Maryland had been talking about. Sooner or later they would assign him a cushy job that allowed him to leave his cell every day and move around so he could see what was what. That was the plan. He would watch for his chance and, when he saw it, he would grab it. Every night, as he lay awake on his prison cot, he smiled in the darkness thinking about the three people in the outside world who had no idea what was coming.

As they rounded a curve on their way back to the Interstate, the overgrown cemetery and the dilapidated trailer next to it reappeared. The boy who had been sitting on the trailer steps was no longer there. About a mile farther down the road Sonny saw him walking on the shoulder. He had nothing with him, no backpack, not even a plastic bag, but Sonny had the feeling that he would never be coming back. As the van approached, the boy turned and raised his thumb.

"Fucking hick," the driver hollered through the open window, and the two guards laughed. The boy raised his finger as the van sped past.

Sonny smiled. He had started out on the same journey a long time ago and, as soon as he got the chance, he was going to finish it. It would be his way of raising a finger to the world one more time.

CHAPTER TWO

The force that would set Sonny free was born name-lessly in the grasslands on the west coast of Africa. It spent the violent night of its birth uprooting the sparse trees of the savannah, separating terrified inhabitants from their helpless huts and setting fire to a laboriously constructed missionary church with the lightning it hurled from a pitch-black sky. Having spent the anger of its youth, the tempest slipped into the Atlantic where it refused to vanish as had the other storms of this particular August. Chosen by some dark lottery of nature, it survived its encounter with the ocean and began growing, sucking life from the sea and swirling to life, slowly becoming a monster.

As it spun wildly across the Atlantic, meteorologists detected its presence on satellite images and began tracking the storm. Being the third disturbance to obtain hurricane wind speeds that season, the storm was given the name Chester. Shipping companies and airlines made note of its existence but saw no great need for alarm since the circular mass on their monitors was still a thousand miles from the nearest inhabited islands and because some of the early computer-generated models of its potential paths showed the system veering north and curling back out into the Atlantic, pushed by winds flowing eastward across North America.

There were those who weren't so sure. Daily satellite updates showed Chester growing at an alarming rate. It was too soon to make an educated call about which path the system would actually take, but if it took one of the more ominous routes generated by National Hurricane Center programs it would rake the Caribbean Islands and draw a deadly bead on the coast of Florida.

Some of those who should have been paying the most attention to the storm's growing threat were not. They were men who fished the Atlantic in small boats that set out each day from the islands in the Caribbean like Turks and Caicos, Crooked Island, and Mayaguana. They had seen news of the storm on the nightly television broadcast from Grand Turk or heard talk of it when they gathered at the end of their long days at places like the Limon Cielo, the bar at the end of the government dock where their boats were tied up. They paid no more attention to the story than they did to the printed health warnings on their cigarette packs or to the frequent admonitions of Fr. Martin about their failure to attend Sunday Mass.

And why should they? The evening seas were calm.

An immense round sun had slipped below the western horizon as they hosed down the decks of their boats and spread nets to dry. The setting sun had been as red as a tomato, and anyone who grew up on the water knew that such a sun was a sure sign of a beautiful morning to follow. Those weathermen are loco, laughed the fishermen as they clicked together their glasses and drank down their rum. There was bait to pay for and gasoline to buy and more children to feed than they wished to remember. They would fish tomorrow and they would fish the next day and the day after that. Each morning, as the rising sun grew paler and fewer gulls followed their boats, the fishermen saw only the fullness of their nets. They returned at night and drank more rum and sang songs of the sea. The rising sun grew still paler, until one morning it came up as white as the host Fr. Martin raised above his head in consecration. The old dog that slept away its days in the town square rose uneasily and dragged itself toward the church, where it squeezed through a missing ventilation grille to the safety of the crawlspace where it had been born.

CHAPTER THREE

The same sun rose each day over the evergreen mountains of East Tennessee, a world away. As it stirred the sleepy town to life it awoke roosters and drew deep shadows beneath the cool overhangs of the only mansion in the town of Mineral City, an imposing edifice constructed of brick by a man who had made a fortune selling lumber.

Virtually the entire front page of the poorly-thrown newspapers littering the town's walkways and lawns was monopolized by eyewitness accounts of the daring rescue of two hysterical teenage girls from the top of the Ferris wheel at the Mineral City Volunteer Fire Department's carnival. A large photograph showed one of the girls in the arms of a helmeted fireman as he made his way down to the ladder truck, an operation that, according to the picture's caption, caused the young lady—a rising sophomore at Mineral City High School—to pass out. Follow-up stories, including an interview with the girl's grandmother, who told the reporter that she had once been rescued from the top of an apple tree, spilled onto the second page. Buried at the bottom of the third page, between an alphabetical listing of persons owing back real estate taxes and an advertisement for the local Goodyear Tire Center, there was a one-paragraph story with the heading *Hurricane Chester Takes Aim at Florida Coast*.

The National Hurricane service today upgraded Chester, a powerful Cape Verde-type storm, to a Category Four Hurricane as winds near its center reached 138 mph. It is currently located 175 miles northwest of Grand Bahama Island and, while forecasters stressed that it is still too early to make a definitive projection, its current course would result in a landfall just north of St. Augustine, Florida. If that projection proves correct, Mineral City residents should brace for heavy rainfall by the end of next week.

If the editors of the *Mineral City Courier* had allocated more space to the report about Hurricane Chester, readers would have been informed that among the first of the more than seventy lives the storm claimed during its deadly sweep through the Caribbean were the crews of two small fishing boats who had become so occupied chasing a large school of amberjack off the coast of Turks and Caicos that they ignored frantic radio transmissions to abandon their nets and run for port. In the days to come there would be those who claimed the crews would have been lost even if they had heeded the warnings, pointing out to reporters from the mainland that the dock where their boats had been kept for generations had been swept out to sea along with the frond-roofed bar at the end of the pier where they drank their rum.

In the Appalachian Mountains where Mineral City was nestled, the weather was perfect and forecast to remain that way for the first part of the new week. The same sun that had arced unseen over the swirling monster in the Atlantic inched its way into a deep blue sky as the residents of the small town yawned and stretched and downed quick cups of coffee. One at a time, and then in a detectable stream, cars backed out of driveways and headed toward the small downtown as the workweek began. The listings in the Mineral City business directory, if there had been such a publication, would have included six law offices, four of them operated by a single lawyer, a franchise grocery store, a 7-Eleven, an Ace Hardware store, and two gasoline stations. The main business in the town, and the surrounding area for that matter, was the prison, a maximum-security facility owned by the Tennessee Department of Corrections but operated by a private contractor, one of several such arrangements in the state.

The prison complex was located on a natural plateau one mile south of the town proper. For security reasons there had been no attempt in its planning or construction to soften with trees or shrubbery the stark image of the unimaginative buildings or the razor wire fencing surrounding them. The only greenery visible from the public road was an expanse of grass between the double fence and the first line of buildings and, by August, even that was no longer green, having been allowed to turn brown and brittle in the summer heat. Though the compound was officially a *corrections facility* it looked exactly like a prison, a fact that didn't seem to bother anyone. The place had been a godsend to the local economy. Most of the town's citizens who had lost their jobs when the last sawmill closed had found employment with the large California corporation that ran the facility. Only a few of those who had been hired had the mentality and temperament to be prison guards. The rest made the most of it. Working at the prison was a steady job, and each morning at eight o'clock the day shift showed their passes at the main gate and fanned out through the complex to begin work.

The guards jokingly referred to the inmates—almost 1,600 of them—as their *clients*. They became friendly with some of them, tolerated most of the rest, and had the good sense to realize that a small percentage of them were as dangerous as the timber rattlesnakes they shot on sight while deer hunting in the mountains above the town.

The most dangerous inmate in the entire prison population was a man named Sonny Masters. He was dangerous because no one realized he was dangerous. Sonny, who had arrived at the facility the previous August, was handsome and affable and spent most of his free time lifting weights. He bothered no one, smiled easily, and called the guards who weren't rule freaks by their first names. There were guards who thought prisoners should speak only when spoken to, and Sonny made no attempt to defy them. He hated the ones who acted that way but he gave no hint that he did, just as he gave no hint that, deep inside, he hated them all. He smiled at the warden, smiled at the idiot chaplain and at the slow-moving maintenance workers, but the smile he greeted them with had no meaning. They were all part of a system that had dumped shit on him since he was old enough to remember, a system that, just two years earlier when he finally had the world by the balls, had taken everything away from him and locked him up like an animal.

The way he acted after they locked him up in Maryland had been a big mistake; Sonny knew that now. He had shown them what they could do with their fucking rules and turned on anyone who even looked at him funny. His last fight had been with the biggest man he had ever seen, a gorilla named Sampson who arrived in the cellblock with the mistaken attitude that he was some kind of a king and that everyone else, including Sonny, had been put on earth to kiss his ass. Even though he had suffered a broken arm and ended up with a face swollen to the size of a basketball, Sonny had beaten the big man to within an inch of his life and, when he was done, he had whispered in his ear that no one is big enough to fuck with Sonny Masters. As it turned out, no one else had a chance to try. The bureaucrats who ran the prison decided that they had seen enough of Sonny Masters and informed the Tennessee Department of Corrections, in a state where he was wanted by the law anyway, that Maryland would accept three of their worst inmates if they would agree to take Sonny.

The people who ran the Mineral City prison didn't get what they were expecting. They read him the riot act when he first arrived and shoved him into solitary for three weeks to give him a taste of what he could expect if he gave them any trouble. Sonny responded to their orders with polite *Yes, sirs* or *No, sirs*. For the first time in his life he was pushed around by other men and did nothing about it. By far the toughest part of his act was pretending to be intimidated by the cellblock tough guys. His natural instinct was to knock their teeth out, but he didn't. He forced a smile, said *Easy, man*, and held up open palms, making it clear that he wanted no trouble. Day in and day out his suppressed rage reached the verge of exploding. It made him sick to do what he was doing, but he did it because it was part of his plan for breaking out and doing the things he wanted to do more than he had ever wanted to do anything in his life.

He needed room to operate. He needed to get a job inside the new prison that would give him the freedom to move around and look for an opening. There had to be a way to escape, and in order to find it he needed a job with the least amount of supervision and the longest leash, the kind of job assigned to the mealy-mouthed *Yes, sir, No, sir* inmates. Doing the things he had to do to get one of those jobs turned Sonny's stomach, but there was no other way. Every night as he lay in his bunk in the disgusting half-light world of body odor and snoring men, he thought about the three of them living free, doing what they wanted to do when they wanted to do

it, two men and a woman who thought they had seen the
last of him. It took every bit of toughness he possessed to
get out of his cot in the morning and say to some punk
guard, *Yes, sir* and *No, sir* and *How was your weekend, Big
Guy* but he did it. From the moment he stepped out of
the van at the Mineral City Maximum Security Facility,
Sonny Masters was a model prisoner. Every guard and
every administrator who came into contact with him
while he was there would swear to that later.

CHAPTER FOUR

———∽∞∽———

Hurricanes were the last thing on anyone's mind five hundred miles north of Mineral City. A string of beautiful days had the people of Hargrove, Maryland, searching for reasons to be outdoors, even if only to wash their cars or cut the grass. T.J. Barnes, the county police chief, was in no hurry to get back to his office and face the pile of paperwork and telephone messages that undoubtedly awaited him. Through his open cruiser window he waved at a county employee who was halfheartedly weed-whacking his way along the fieldstone wall that marked the entrance to Cattail Creek Park. Giving in to the temptation to enjoy a little sunshine, T.J. hit his left turn signal, swung into the park, and drove through the shaded tunnel of ancient oaks to the little piece of heaven where he had spent half the days of his youth.

Off to his left, wide green fields lined Cattail Creek and the lake where T.J. had learned to swim. He drove slowly to the parking lot at the end of the long driveway and saw that every space in sight was taken, mostly by family station wagons and the SUVs that were making station wagons obsolete. Out of habit he glanced at the tags of the vehicles parked in handicapped spaces and noted that most of them were violations. If he were in the mood he could have written a book full of tickets and generated a nice chunk of change for the county. But, since he was rarely in that mood, he moved on. Every one of those vehicles, he rationalized, belonged to people who were spending time with their kids, and that was all the reason he needed to cut them a little slack. It was a way of thinking that would have been totally beyond the comprehension of the revenue-hungry county council members, not to mention the county executive, Fat Frank Riley, who T.J. regarded as the biggest horse's ass who had ever come down the pike. He smiled and declared, in Fat Frank's honor, a one-day parking-violation holiday for anyone using Cattail Creek Park.

He drove around the far end of the playing fields, pulled up onto the grass near the lake, and cut his engine. The sight framed by his windshield seemed like a picture of what life in this world was supposed to be. The field of grass with its grid of chalked lines was overrun with squealing kids, half of them in bright yellow shirts and the other half dressed in grasshopper-green, chasing an elusive white ball. Some of their parents lined the field, gesturing and jumping up and down wildly while just as many lounged in clusters of lawn chairs watching smaller children play games of their own. T.J. could never have put what he was thinking into words that didn't sound stupid, but to him that didn't matter. He was perfectly comfortable saying to himself that protecting what he was looking at right now, these good people and this kind of place, was why he had become a policeman in the first place. It was the reason he put up with the never-ending hassle of dealing with politicians who expected his police department to keep the county free of thugs and drugs and as peaceful as a Sunday picnic on a budget that was at least five years out of date.

"Hey, Bobby, how's it going?" T.J. called as he left his cruiser and strolled over to the sideline where a very bald and very tanned man was trying his best to keep a gaggle of squealing kids from running amok. "I assume that whistle around your neck means you're in charge here."

"Oh yeah. That's why they pay me the big bucks."

Bobby Santoro and T.J. Barnes had known each other since the days when they rode their bikes a good three miles each way to this very park in the freezing cold of winter to practice football and in the sweltering heat of summer to swim in the lake. A few of their contemporaries, the ones who lived farther away, were lucky enough to be driven to the park, but not even their parents stayed to spectate in those days.

"I didn't know you were a soccer fan."

"I'm not," T.J. replied, "I didn't even know anyone played soccer in the middle of the summer."

"It's not a league, just one of the camps the county

has for everything these days: soccer camp, golf camp, field hockey camp, you name it. Just like when we were kids, right?"

"Right." They both laughed.

The kids who were clustered around Bobby gawked at T.J. the way they usually did when they were close to him, fascinated—and probably a little nervous—about his size and his uniform and, of course, his gun. All he ever knew to do in these situations was smile and say hello. Some of them said hello back but mostly they pressed closer to Bobby, who reacted with a smile and glanced up at the sky.

"Soccer camp is supposed to run for another week. I hope we get it in before that storm they're talking about moves up the coast."

T.J. had seen a report on television about the storm and the terrible devastation it had caused on some island in the Caribbean, but he hadn't heard anything yet from the State Emergency Management Agency and, with everything else he had on his plate, he wasn't going to worry about it until he did. He patted his old friend on the back and was about to leave when a boy wearing a soccer shirt at least one size too big for him slipped quietly up to Bobby and tugged at his arm.

"Noah, where have you been? The game is half-over!"

Hearing the name caused T.J. to take a good look at the boy. He was quite a bit taller than the last time T.J. had seen him, but there was no doubt in T.J.'s mind who he was or who his mother was. In her tight jeans and high-heeled shoes Sandra Lucas was easy enough to spot, leaning butt-first against the hood of a car with her arms crossed.

"Get in there and tell number twenty in the yellow shirt to come out for a little while," Bobby told the boy, shoving him gently toward the playing field. Noah hesitated, glanced up at T.J., then headed uncertainly toward the screaming mass of boys and girls.

"He seemed to know you. I hope he doesn't have a record," Bobby laughed.

T.J. shook his head and motioned for his friend to step away from the circle of kids so they could talk. "Noah Lucas. His mother was involved with Sonny Masters when he killed that old man out at the old Dixon place where she was living at the time. That poor kid saw the whole thing."

Bobby shook his head. "I remember that business. Masters threatened to kill you when he got out of prison, didn't he?"

"They all do."

That was a bit of an exaggeration, but T.J. didn't want anyone to worry about Sonny Masters. The man was gone and would be gone for a long time, doing the fifteen years in prison for manslaughter that he had been sentenced to up here and an additional fifteen years for attacking, and doing considerable damage to, the three Tennessee state troopers who had brought his flight from Maryland to an end.

Bobby lowered his voice and gestured toward the

field where Noah had disappeared into the squealing mob of green and yellow shirts. "He swore he was going to kill that boy's mother too, didn't he?"

"And that guy from Richmond who jumped him when he was selling cars for Randall Phillips."

"You worried?" Bobby asked.

T.J. shook his head. "If Sonny Masters doesn't get himself killed in prison, he will be an old man by the time he's free again." He pointed toward the field. "You better pay attention to what's going on out there. That doesn't look like any sport I've ever seen."

Bobby laughed then blew his whistle. "Guys! Hey, guys!"

"Hello, Mrs. Lucas," T.J. said as casually as he could manage when he got back to his cruiser.

Noah's mother nodded—at least, T.J. believed it was a nod—but she didn't smile. "This was the only place left to park. I was hoping that police car didn't belong to you."

Sandra Lucas had never said a warm word to T.J. in the two years that had passed since he tried to warn her about the man she was dating, an intervention she strongly resented at the time and had obviously never gotten over. As far as he could tell it made no difference to her that that same violent person, an animal with a record of preying on women when he wasn't beating up people in barrooms, ended up killing a seventy-one-year-old man right in front of her son before trying to drag her away with him. T.J. had given up trying to understand why she couldn't see that all he had been trying to do was protect her and her boy. It wasn't like he expected her to jump up and down every time they met, but it would have made running into her a hell of a lot more pleasant if she lightened up a little and made an effort to turn the page.

He gave it one more try. "That boy of yours is really sprouting up."

Sandra Lucas yawned, checked her fingernails, and—giving no indication that she had heard him—glanced toward the soccer field.

T. J touched the brim of his hat and slipped behind the wheel of the big Ford. He rolled down the windows and was about to start his engine when the quiet lake dispatched a warm breeze to remind him of its presence. For a second, but only a second, he thought about the pile of papers on his desk back at the station, then slipped back out of the cruiser, tapped the brim of his hat again to Sandra Lucas, and walked slowly to the edge of the water. By habit, he looked for the rope swing that he and his friends had once used by the hour. The same massive oak tree was still there, one muscular arm extended high above the lake, but the rope was long gone, a victim of an extensive safety evaluation conducted by the county's insurance carrier years ago, the same callous review that had eliminated sliding boards from elementary school playgrounds and mandated that tackle football be elimi-

25

nated from the list of sports the recreation department was permitted to offer to kids younger than thirteen, an age by which T.J. and Bobby and all the others he grew up with had been playing tackle for six years. And with no ill effects, T.J. thought to himself, at least not until he played at the University of Maryland and wrecked his knee his senior year in the NC State game, an injury that reminded him of its presence whenever rain was on the way. The fact that it was aching this morning struck T.J. as strange; he looked up and saw that the only clouds in the deep blue sky above the park looked like drifting cotton balls.

A tanned girl sitting high in a lifeguard chair waved. She was a very pretty girl, brown as a bean, whose mother worked at the courthouse.

"Hello, Melissa, saved anybody yet today?"

"Not yet, but I'm ready." She flexed her arm muscles, and T.J. laughed. There had been no lifeguards at the lake back when T.J. and his friends rode their bikes to the park and spent entire summer days in the water, just a rusting sign that read, "Swim At Your Own Risk." And they did. Not to mention climbing twenty feet up in that old oak tree and launching themselves far out into the lake, screaming like a bunch of deranged Tarzans. He was glad he had been a kid in those days. No parents in folding lawn chairs watching their every move and no lifeguards, even if they were as pretty as this one, to tell them that the things they were doing were against the rules.

"Keep an eye on me. I'm going to walk out along the dam to see how it's holding up."

"You're braver than me," the young lifeguard replied, dabbing white cream onto her sunburned nose. "My girl-friend saw a snake sunning on those rocks the other day."

T.J. promised with a smile that he would be careful and started out along the wide stone dam behind which the lake had formed a hundred years ago. It wasn't his responsibility to perform safety inspections, but there had been a presentation at a county council meeting a few months back that he couldn't get out of his mind. The Public Works Department had commissioned an engineering firm to examine the ancient dam and make a report on its condition. Using slides illustrating each point addressed in the handouts given to members of the council as well as to the county commissioner, a young engineer had made it clear that the deteriorating structure was in need of immediate attention in order to keep the five-acre lake behind it from breaking loose and thundering down the streambed toward the old bridge on Baltimore Road and into two large subdivi-sions a half mile below the bridge. With the earnestness of youth and the responsibility of what might well have been his first major assignment, the engineer referred to records indicating that the dam had been built out of stone gathered from nearby fields by the operator of a long-abandoned gristmill. He flashed illustrations onto the council's new high-tech projection screen detailing that all of the construction had taken place without the mortar and steel reinforcement required by present-day code requirements.

Fat Frank Riley, the county executive, had interrupted at that point. "Young man, that dam has been in its present location since—what do I see in your report, 1885?—and the last time I looked the lake hadn't gone anywhere." He tossed his copy of the report into the pile of papers in front of him. "We will take this information under advisement and let the director of public works know if we feel that any action is required."

"Yes, sir," the young engineer had answered, obviously alarmed that the report into which he had put so much effort had not generated the concern he had anticipated. "But, if you will refer to page nineteen you will see that the structure depends solely on the mass of the stones for its strength and has been gradually losing that mass as individual stones break free and tumble into the downstream creek bed."

"Tumble," Fat Frank had chuckled. "On that note we are going to *tumble* along with our agenda. Thank you, Mr. . . ." When he hesitated one of the two lackeys positioned behind his chair whispered in the county executive's ear. "Yes. Thank you, Mr. Cole. That will be all."

And that had ended all discussion about the old dam. At that same meeting the council approved funding to lease new cars for the executive and all five council members and to rebuild the greens at the municipal golf course where Fat Frank played when he couldn't weasel an invitation to play at the country club. For the third straight meeting the council turned down T.J.'s request to replace the ancient electrical generator at the police station and refused to provide the funds for hiring two additional officers.

T.J. saw no snakes sunning on the rough-hewn rectangular stones as he made his way out to the middle of the dam. What he did see, because he was looking for it, was the growing accumulation of loose stone near the downstream base of the wall. It all appeared harmless enough; in fact, the sight of the creek spinning lazily through the pile of rubble only added to the calendar-like reflection of the roofless and vine-tangled gristmill on the far side of Cattail Creek.

How much water did the big lake behind him hold? What had that young engineer said? He couldn't remember exactly, but it was some incredible figure. He picked up a small rock that was lodged between two of the big stones at his feet and started to throw it into the creek a good fifteen feet below the dam. At the last second he hesitated, put the rock back where he'd found it and wedged it firmly into place with his boot. For all he knew that small rock was all that was holding the whole damn thing together. He didn't really believe that, but he wasn't taking any chances.

Before he turned to leave T.J. took one last look down into the creek. Even to a person as observant as he was, the strange restlessness of the water went unnoticed.

CHAPTER FIVE

In Mineral City, Tennessee, there had not been a single bird in the sky all morning, a rare phenomenon that the guards who were supposed to be supervising the recycling detail were no more likely to notice than the blue skies of other days or the wildflowers that grew boldly along the high steel fence that defined their workday world. Under an ominously dark sky, three of them huddled on the prison loading dock, one of the few places in the sprawling facility where they could smoke without getting caught.

"Just look at that goddamned thing, will you," the guard named McNulty exclaimed, pointing with his cigarette at the huge emergency generator that had just been installed no more than twenty feet from where they were standing. "Looks like a cross between a locomotive and a bulldozer."

Final hookup of the bright-yellow monstrosity had

been completed late the previous day. A demonstration for the prison maintenance staff was scheduled for the following day but, as the warden had been assured, the new generator was already programmed to fire up every electrical system in the complex in the event of a power failure.

"What's in that huge tank next to it?"

"Coal gas, enough fuel to keep that monster running for a week. Johnson told me it's only temporary until the underground tank gets here."

McNulty was talking about Randall Johnson, the prison's lethargic facilities manager, a man who had been repeatedly directed by his bosses at corporate head-quarters in California to replace an outdated generator that had failed the last two state inspections. The last directive had been in the form of an ultimatum: have the new generator in place and running in two weeks or clean out your desk. The job had been done. Almost. The underground fuel tank was on back order, an extremely important piece of information that Randall Johnson omitted from his report to the home office. Understand-ably omitted from the same report was the fact that the temporary surface tank, filled to the brim with extremely flammable coal oil, was a blatant safety code violation. Both the state and federal investigations that followed its disastrous explosion would uncover evidence that, in return for temporary approval of the vulnerable tank, two electrical inspectors had been significantly enriched by funds from Randall Johnson's operating budget.

Officer McNulty looked down the long driveway toward the main gate and, unaware that the huge cylindrical fuel tank was as dangerous as an unexploded bomb, flicked the remains of his cigarette toward the new equipment. "Let's get the recycling crew moving. Here comes the truck."

"Let's go, Masters," McNulty barked, poking his head through the loading dock door. "Get out there and do whatever the driver tells you to do. You goldbrick or cause trouble on my shift and this will be your first day *and* your last day on this detail."

Sonny nodded and smiled at the big-eared guard who was universally known throughout the prison as *Br'er Rabbit,* a nickname he responded to by filing exaggerated disciplinary reports about any inmate he even suspected of using it.

"I'll be right in there watching you," McNulty announced, nodding toward the small office with a window facing the loading dock. "Let me know if he gives you any trouble," he shouted at the driver who was busy connecting a steel ramp to the rear of the truck. "Yeah, yeah," the man replied without looking up.

Sonny wasn't going to give McNulty anything to watch. All he wanted to do his first few times out on the dock was get an idea of what went on when the recycling trucks were loaded; that and making a buddy out of the driver. A plan might come to him in a week; it might come to him in a month; it might take longer than that, but he wasn't going to do a thing until he had it all worked out. He glanced up at the camera mounted above the loading dock door then looked away quickly, realizing that he didn't want the guard monitoring the security screens to wonder what he was curious about.

The truck driver stood and wiped his sweating forehead with a red paisley bandana that made him look like a country hick. Sonny nodded at him and said, "Hey."

"Yeah, yeah," the driver replied as he studied the strange black sky. "It's going to rain like shit. Let's get moving."

They went into the sorting room where Sonny had worked for the previous two months, keeping his mouth shut and busting his butt. The two guards watching the sorters glanced his way then quickly resumed an argument about the relative merits of Ford and Chevy pickup trucks. "You're full of shit," one of them informed the other. "Chevys are for old ladies."

Sonny and the driver began rolling carts of separated materials onto the loading dock. From behind his small window McNulty watched them run the first one up the ramp onto the truck then slipped a copy of *Shotgun News* out of his jacket and began thumbing through it, oblivious to the growing rumble of thunder and the strange coil of dark clouds that had slithered down the mountain and settled over the valley.

Sonny paid no attention to the sky or to the strangely

waning daylight. As he loaded the truck his attention was focused on the driveway running downhill from the loading dock to the main gate. Silently, he measured the distance and made a mental note that, since there was no guardhouse next to it, the gate opening out onto the public road must be electronically monitored. These were things he would have to think about carefully. He refused to let his mind run wild, fighting off an insane urge to jump into the huge truck and use it like a giant battering ram to obliterate the gate. While his heart raced with fantasies of freedom, he pushed another cart up the ramp, where the driver grabbed it impatiently and shoved it deep into the cavernous vehicle. Before Sonny could retrieve another cart a blinding bolt of lightning struck so close to the loading dock that the earsplitting explosion of thunder it produced was instantaneous.

"That's it for me," the driver yelled toward the window behind which McNulty was sitting. "They don't pay me enough to get my ass blown off by lightning!" He jumped from the back of the truck onto the dock and began disassembling the portable ramp.

McNulty hurried out of his office waving his arms. "Where the hell do you think you are going?" he screamed through the roar of a wind that had come out of nowhere. "You got sixteen more carts to load!"

"I'll be goddamned!"

Heavy raindrops smacked the concrete loading dock as the remaining morning light surrendered to the strange clouds, and thunder and lightning laid siege to the prison compound. Driveway lights went dark, blinked back on, then died. Seconds later, every light in the prison complex went dark, causing the mighty generator to cough to life. The wall speaker above the loading dock cleared its throat in a burst of static. "Guards return all inmates to their cellblocks immediately. Repeat, guards return all inmates to their cellblocks immediately."

"Get those carts into the sorting room on the double, Masters!" McNulty bellowed. "You heard the announcement!"

The driver slammed the last of the loading ramp into the slot above the recycling truck's massive rear bumper just as the two sorting room guards came out onto the loading dock. "Everything okay, McNulty?"

"Hell yeah, everything is okay! Get your inmates back to the cellblock! I've got Masters!"

A gust of wind swept across the dock, sending McNulty's hat spinning into the ankle-deep water swirling around the truck's rear tires.

"Get your ass down there and find that hat!" the guard ordered Sonny.

Before Sonny could move, lightning struck high on the wall behind the generator, hurling shattered bricks and mortar in every direction.

"I said get down there and find my fucking hat!" McNulty screamed, drawing his weapon.

Sonny glanced at the other two guards, who had frozen in the doorway when McNulty drew his gun. Like twins striking an identical pose, they stood with one hand on their holstered weapons and the other on their hats, with eyes half-closed against the blinding wind-driven rain. McNulty, in an irrational rage about losing his hat, pointed his weapon at Sonny. "I'm not telling you again, Masters!"

Sonny jumped off the dock, landing beside the truck's train-like tandem of oversized steel wheels and heavy-duty tires, cover enough to shield him from the flying shards of metal that exploded through the air no more than a second later, decapitating McNulty and dismembering the truck driver and both sorting room guards. A blinding lightning strike had scored a direct hit on the coal oil fuel tank, setting off an explosion that sent debris flying like shrapnel and leaving the prison in total darkness. Fragments of steel, some the size of a car engine, ripped loose from the generator and rocketed across the loading dock, digging up chunks of concrete and obliterating a steel handrail before caroming under the recycling truck and narrowly missing Sonny's legs as he dashed toward the driver's door.

In the rapid-fire flashes of lightning that followed the explosion Sonny saw the keys in the ignition, the last breach of prison procedure that the truck driver would ever commit. Sonny was halfway into the cab when a blue-white bolt of lightning exposed a handgun in a mass of spiraling blood on the overflowing pavement. When he jumped down and grabbed the gun, the remains of a hand dropped free and spun slowly toward an overwhelmed storm drain. Sonny was too focused to be sickened or startled. He wiped the gun clean with his bare hand, rubbed his hand against the rain-slick fender of the truck, and jumped up into the driver's seat. His mind was fixed on a single thought: *There would never in a thousand years be another chance like this.*

With the generator blown, Sonny knew there would be chaos inside the prison. He pictured panicked guards groping for the emergency lockers where their flashlights were stored. He pictured inmates taking advantage of the unexpected darkness to even scores with their favorite guards. Until the cellblocks were back under control, time was on his side. He started the truck and pulled it into gear. Some of the tires were flat, he realized that immediately, but, like a wounded buffalo, the mammoth recycling truck began to roll toward the distant gate. Sonny's instinct was to not turn on the headlights, but it was either that or drive blind. The truck gained speed, rolling through the torrential rain while Sonny fumbled to locate the windshield wiper control. Between the wipers flapping at full speed and the salvos of lightning that relit the day for seconds at a time, he zeroed in on his target at the end of the long driveway. The accelerator remained pushed all the way to the floor until the giant vehicle reached the gate and destroyed it in a violent eruption of pipe, mesh, and barbed wire that, on any other day, would have been heard a mile away. On this day it was masked completely by the thunderous storm.

CHAPTER SIX

The driver of the dark-green Gardner Plumbing and Heating van slammed on his brakes, skidding to a stop just short of the recycling truck as it swerved out of the prison grounds. Sonny jumped out of the truck and ran toward the van, waving the handgun.

"Get the hell out of there and give me the keys!" Sonny screamed, pounding on the driver's window with the butt of the gun.

The man was so occupied swiping away the hot coffee he had spilled into his lap that he only half heard Sonny's demand. Sonny pulled open the door, stuck the gun in the man's face, and repeated his words.

"My boss will kill me if I give you this van!"

"And I'm going to kill you if you don't!"

The driver, his wide eyes now focused on the gun, slipped slowly from behind the wheel.

"Now, give me your wallet and strip off that jacket!"

Switching the handgun from one hand to the other, Sonny worked the Gardner Plumbing and Heating jacket over his prison shirt. He studied the man, trying to decide what to do with him, then, for no other reason than that he was now free to do anything he felt like doing, Sonny shot him in the chest and watched him slide to the flooded pavement.

The jacket fit fine. Sonny zipped it up against the rain as he peered calmly back toward the prison. Black smoke billowed from the loading dock area, but he was too far away to see any more than that. He thought about blocking the end of the driveway with the recycling truck but decided that a much smarter idea was to get his ass moving. He jumped into the van, swerved around the big truck, and took off into the storm, running over the dead man lying in the road. If he noticed the sickening one-two jolt of both sets of wheels crushing the lifeless body, it didn't affect his concentrated effort to see the road through the pelting rain.

Euphoria bordering on madness seized Sonny as he raced along the twisting country road leading away from the hell of prison and toward three people who had no idea the collector was on his way. Like the storm that had come out of nowhere and set him free, he would sweep back into their lives, leave two of them dead and the other one wishing she was dead. It didn't matter what happened after that. If he got away with it, fine. If he didn't, that was fine too. The important thing was that they would pay the way people who messed with Sonny Masters had always paid. He had been settling scores since he was a boy, and for the past two years, the thought of anyone owing him as much as these three did had almost driven him crazy.

Night after night, lying awake on his prison bunk, he had dealt with each of them in their special ways, coming upon them unannounced and seeing the initial shock in their eyes turn to desperation when they realized that Sonny Masters held all the cards this time around. Night after night he had driven these roads—roads that he knew as well as anyone because he had grown up in this part of the country. He had not known how he would elude the police; he had only known that he would. He had not known exactly how he would escape, only that it would happen one way or another. His plans for breaking out had been elaborate, schemes that would take months, a year if necessary. Never in all those nights of planning had he envisioned the dumb luck that had come his way today. Not once had he counted on day turning into night or explosions of lightning like he had never seen in his life blasting a pathway to freedom. Only a fool would have counted on things like that, but the fact was that those things had happened, and when they did Sonny Masters had done what he had done his entire life: he had grabbed opportunity by the balls and run with it.

Until this day, life had pissed all over him. Without

realizing he was doing it, Sonny squeezed the steering wheel of the van so tightly that his fingers grew numb. He pressed down on the accelerator; cursing a childhood he had done nothing to deserve, cursing the rusting trailer propped precariously on a hillside in West Tennessee where as a small boy he had to choose between sleeping outside in the freezing woods or risk being beaten half to death for no better reason than that his drunken father was tired of slapping his mother around. Because he knew no better, he had thought that starting school would allow him to escape for at least a part of the day. He could not have been more wrong. From the first morning of the first day of school his tattered clothes and beat-up shoes became the targets of his classmates' gleeful mockery. They descended on him as though he were some kind of strange animal that had wandered onto their playground. The teachers had not been much better, mildly rebuking his tormentors but treating him with disdain that even a small child could recognize. By the end of the first week of school he stopped hoping that they would leave him alone and, as time passed, his skin grew thick and his heart became cold and hard. He came to hate all of them and began wishing secretly that the school building would burn to the ground, killing everyone but him, or that the school bus would be hit by a train at the grade crossing near the paper mill while he jumped to safety.

Thinking about that school bus caused him to drive even faster. He leaned closer to the windshield and tried to concentrate on seeing through the blinding rain. If life on the playground or in the classroom was bad, riding on the bus in the morning and again in the afternoon was even worse. The other kids, kids who lived in houses with white fences and neat lawns, made up a song that they sang every day on the bus—a song about a boy who lived in a trailer and wore funny clothes.

> *Hole in Sonny's shirtsleeve,*
> *Hole in Sonny's shoe,*
> *Smells like a monkey, smells like a zoo.*

They laughed and squealed and pointed at him while Percy Spence, the bus driver, did nothing but glance up into the big rearview mirror and grin at him with his crooked brown teeth. Sometimes Sonny could see Mr. Spence's lips moving with the cruel words that amused them all so much. He was dead now, old Percy was, his brains blown out a week after Sonny got thrown out of the Army. He had begged Sonny not to shoot him, swearing on his mother's grave that he had just been having a little fun, but his pathetic pleas had made no difference to Sonny. Mr. Spence owed a debt, and Sonny Masters had come collecting.

Two headlights pierced the silver-gray downpour and bore down on Sonny. Before he could react, what appeared to be a white sports car swerved across his path, clipped the front bumper of the van, and vanished into the unearthly darkness. Sonny fought to stay on the road, careening to the left then overcorrecting to the right, where he bounced wildly along a guardrail before catching sight of the double yellow center line and regaining control. He held his breath, waiting for a tire to go flat or to feel some other sign of damage that would leave him stranded in the middle of nowhere. Seconds passed, then a minute. He heard nothing and he felt nothing and, as he sped back up, he exploded in anger. "You son of a bitch!" he screamed at the unknown driver who had almost ruined everything. "I hope your sorry ass is at the bottom of the mountain in a thousand fucking pieces!"

It took Sonny a few minutes to calm down and refocus. He was heading north, he was sure of that, and at some point, if the rain let up enough, he would see a sign for Interstate 81. All he had to do was follow the plan he had worked out a thousand times in his mind, and, according to that plan, the fun would start at an apartment building just outside of Richmond, Virginia, where the father of an old girlfriend lived. Sonny couldn't wait. "That bastard Maury probably laughs himself to sleep every night thinking about what he did to me," Sonny whispered to the empty seat beside him. "Well, you son of a bitch, you're about to find out what happens to people who mess with Sonny Masters." Vivid images of giving Maury Workman what he had coming to him were interrupted by a vibration coming from the van's front end.

Sonny held his breath as he felt a rhythmic shaking of the steering wheel that told him all he needed to know: he was going to have to ditch the van and get another vehicle. At precisely that moment a large green sign appeared, phantom-like, above the road. The blinding rain made it almost unreadable, but Sonny was sure he saw the Interstate symbol and the number 81. He laughed out loud. This was his day.

By the time he reached the exit he knew what he was going to do next. He would pass the northbound ramp and head south, away from Richmond, until he came to a motel where he could park the van and steal a car. Once they no longer had their hands full with the storm, every cop in the state would be looking for him, and he loved the idea of them finding the Gardner Plumbing and Heating van pointing in the wrong direction. Sonny was the fox and they were the hunters. The thought gave him a thrill.

CHAPTER SEVEN

In Richmond, news of the storm worked its way onto the front page of the *Times-Dispatch* and became the lead story of every network report. In suburban Henrico County, Maury Workman, a retired crane operator, shooed a large black cat from his favorite chair and sat down to watch television. He settled a Diet Coke on the coffee table in front of him and lit a cigarette as the cat bounded into his lap. "Buckeye, old buddy," he said to the cat, "Let's you and me check out the news and see if we have enough time left to build ourselves a lifeboat."

He watched as the focus of the report shifted from the massive storm damage in the Bahamas to satellite images of the path the swirling giant had taken through the southern Atlantic as it bore down on the United States. Florida and Georgia had taken it on the chin, sustaining more damage than they had from any storm since the havoc and devastation wrought by Hurricane Andrew in

1992. The governors of states as far north as Connecticut had already put the National Guard on alert while the Red Cross and local emergency services prepared for a potential disaster. As skies darkened, beaches had been closed along the coast, cutting short vacations from the Outer Banks to Virginia Beach. In towns big and small, citizens were being urged to prepare for the worst.

Coverage switched to a parka–clad reporter on a windy beach near Hilton Head. Maury looked around for the television remote so he could turn down the sound of the wind roaring through the reporter's microphone. As he did, his eye settled on the gold-framed photograph of a beautiful young woman on the coffee table. The racket on the television grew distant as he took the picture of his daughter, Susan, into his hands. She no longer looked like this—not the left side of her face anyway, not since the last beating she had suffered at the hands of an animal named Sonny Masters. It wasn't the first time he had hit her, both Maury and his late wife Laura had been sure about that, but it was by far the worst he had ever hurt her. Maury had been a lightweight boxer when he was in the Navy. He had seen a lot of guys get beat up, both in the ring and in barrooms, but he had never seen anyone as battered as his little girl. She wouldn't talk about it after it happened, either to them or to the police, and— what was totally beyond Maury's understanding—she got angry whenever they said anything bad about Sonny, swearing she loved him and would always love him no matter what anyone said about him.

The picture in his hands had been taken before Sonny beat her up, making it a little easier for Maury to remember her the way he wanted to remember her. It had taken months, but Susan recovered enough to go back to work teaching, telling everyone she had been injured in an automobile accident. Thanks to two operations, her nose looked almost the same as had before the beating, but not even the specialists had been able to do anything with her left eye, the one she had almost lost. It was nerve damage, they said, that caused the eyelid to sag the way it did and for the one side of her face to always look tired. She was still beautiful; he could never admit to himself that she wasn't, because it hurt too much.

There was a second picture on the coffee table, one of his wife, Laura, that had been taken when she was roughly Susan's age. Everyone had always said she looked like Tammy Wynette, a compliment that pleased her more than she would ever admit. Laura was gone now, gone for just over a year, taken out of the blue by a heart attack right before her sixtieth birthday. Her doctor said he thought her heart might have had an undetected congenital defect, but Maury knew better. Laura had never been the same after seeing the horrible way Sonny had beaten her only child; she never slept more than three hours at a time, she lost weight, and she started smoking again, something she hadn't done since she was in her twenties. As far as Maury was concerned, Sonny Masters had not only disfigured his beautiful daughter, he had also killed his wife.

On television, a woman who looked more like she was modeling clothes than reporting the news posed in front of a map of the eastern United States. Hurricane Chester had made landfall approximately fifty miles north of St. Augustine, Florida, she stated with a tooth-paste smile that seemed out of place, and then curved northward as predicted. The huge system, a swirling mass of yellow and red on her map, was tracking east of the Appalachian Mountains as it made its way through the Carolinas, where building supply stores had sold out of plywood, duct tape, flashlights, and portable generators. Grocery stores, she added, strutting toward the camera, were selling milk, bread, and bottled water faster than they could restock their shelves.

Maury took a swig of the Diet Coke and gently pushed the protesting cat from his lap. "Need something a little stronger than this soft drink, Buckeye. I'll be right back." The cat followed him into the kitchen and rubbed against his legs as he stared through the window over the sink. It was raining and, against the heavy sky, a small flock of white birds fought their way through the wind toward distant trees. He found the bottle and poured out some of the Coke to make room for whiskey.

There was one thing about the whole sorry mess that made Maury feel good every time he thought about it. About six months after Sonny Masters beat up his daughter he had driven to Maryland to attend the funeral of a guy he had boxed with in the Navy and, while he was up there, the water pump on his pickup truck had gone out. The next day, as he was returning a loaner car to the dealer who had done the repair—he raised his drink to the rain-streaked window as he remembered a scene that was like something out of a movie—Sonny Masters himself strolled across the parking lot, looking like he owned the damn place. Just as Maury was about to tromp on the accelerator and run over the bastard, he realized that, if he did it that way, Sonny would never know what hit him or why. He wanted the bastard to see his face. He wanted him to feel pain and know where it came from. Sonny was a full head taller than Maury and a hell of a lot younger, but Maury had fought a lot of bigger men both in and out of the ring. He jumped out of the car and, before Sonny knew what was happening, kicked him in the balls as hard as he could and went after him with the fists of a madman. Maury would have hit him all day long if a couple of mechanics had not dragged him away. What he had done that morning could in no way erase what Sonny had done to his daughter; but it was one of the highlights of his life.

Maury opened the refrigerator to check his supplies. His wife, Laura, had been a very good cook but, except for the rare occasions when he picked up something at Subway, he had lived on bologna sandwiches since she died. Not just any bologna sandwiches; Oscar Meyer bologna, Hellmann's mayonnaise, and a little lettuce on Wonder Bread, the way Laura made them. "Looks like I have enough food for a few days, and there's plenty of cat food in the pantry. Bring on Hurricane What's-His-

49

Name, Buckeye. We're ready." The cat followed Maury back into the living room and jumped into his lap the second he sat back down.

Not long after returning home from his trip to Maryland, Maury learned that Sonny Masters had been arrested for going into a rage and killing a man who was in his seventies, an act of violence that had delighted Maury, not because of what Sonny had done to that poor guy, but because it meant Sonny was finally going to prison where he belonged. Maury had been subpoenaed to testify about what Sonny had done to his daughter; testimony he never gave because the judge ruled it had nothing to do with the manslaughter charge Sonny was being tried for. He could have driven back to Richmond right then and there, but he didn't. The sight of Sonny sitting in the hot seat with armed policemen watching his every move gave him so much pleasure that he checked into a motel and went to the trial every day, making sure that he sat where Sonny could see him. His favorite part of the entire trial was when their eyes met and he gave Sonny the finger by pretending to scratch his ear. For a few seconds he thought Sonny was going to come right out of his chair. Maury had laughed quietly to himself, and all Sonny could do about it was look at him with the cold stare of a snake.

It was the same look that Maury remembered Sonny directing at the local police chief up there, a man named Barnes, as the officer recited from memory the dates and locations of the many barroom brawls that Sonny had been involved in since he moved into the county. "Your Honor," the police chief had concluded, "Mr. Masters's claim that he killed Mr. Tucker in self-defense is absurd. In the last reported incident involving Mr. Masters"—he looked down at his notes to verify the date and time— "approximately twenty-four hours before Mr. Tucker was killed, Sonny Masters was involved in a fight at a bar in this county named the Starlight Lounge. The man he fought, a thirty-eight-year-old biker weighing approximately three hundred pounds, was taken to St. Joseph's Hospital with five missing teeth, four broken ribs, and a lacerated kidney." Chief Barnes paused and glared at Sonny Masters. "On the other hand, Ben Tucker, the victim in this case, was a one hundred and seventy–pound man in his seventies." Maury had liked Police Chief Barnes, a man who he believed would have liked nothing better than to step outside the courthouse with Sonny Masters right then and there and skip all the trouble of holding a trial. "That's one fight I would have paid to see, Buckeye." The cat looked up at him, stretched, and went back to sleep.

A television reporter in a bright yellow slicker fought to keep from being blown sideways by the wind as, far behind him, the angry sea relentlessly attacked a wind-swept beach. The image on the screen switched to what looked like the inside of a warehouse where two splintered boards were propped up against a cinder-block wall. Several carved letters on one of the boards appeared to be the beginning of a word.

"These wood fragments washed up on the beach here in the Bahamas early this morning. We are told by the Coast Guard that they are, in all probability, the remains of the transom—or the back—of the type of fishing boats used in these islands." The reporter paused dramatically. "We can only imagine the fate of this boat's crew or of the crews on a number of other fishing boats that have not been heard from since the full force of Hurricane Chester hammered this part of the Atlantic."

The camera moved in for a close-up of one of the transom boards and lingered on the carved letters that had been painted gold against the bright blue of what was left of the wood. The first letter was clearly a capital "S" and the second was a small "A." The third letter may have been a small "N," but only one corner of it showed. The camera lingered on the only clues to the lost boat's identity until the yellow-slickered reporter returned to the screen long enough to say, "Back to you, Renee."

Maury Workman surfed through the channels with the television remote until he found a *Gunsmoke* rerun. "All we can do about this storm, Buckeye, is hunker down and hope the roof of this apartment building doesn't blow right off."

Chapter Eight

A hundred and fifty miles farther north, T.J. Barnes sat at his kitchen table stirring his second cup of coffee, something he did by habit even though he never used cream or sugar. His father had done the same thing, swearing that coffee tasted better when stirred regardless of whether a person put anything in it or not.

T.J. removed the spoon and watched the small whirlpool in the cup slow, then disappear. He took a sip and then a swallow, staring through the rain-streaked window. The lights in Verna Olsen's windows appeared to flicker off and on as the thick stand of trees at the far end of his property swayed in the growing wind. He knew Verna had been up for hours, finished her usual breakfast of one egg sunny side up with a small piece of fried ham, washed the dishes, and was more than likely sitting at her kitchen table, thumbing through a cookbook whose pages were stained with the faded splashes of ingredients and most of whose recipes had been corrected and embellished in her small, neat handwriting. *One egg is plenty! Use brown sugar instead. 350° burns the bottom crust.* The cookbook was older than T.J., a fact Verna had pointed out to him innumerable times, and far more useful, she had declared more than once when he was a boy. One thing T.J. knew for sure was that whatever she decided to put in her oven today would make that big old house beyond the trees smell as wonderful as a bakery. Thinking about Verna reminded T.J. that it had been a few days since he had checked on her, an oversight that, because of everything that was going on right now, would have to go uncorrected a little bit longer.

It was going to be a long day. Bad weather meant malfunctioning traffic lights, snarled traffic, and a slew of fender benders. His department, already so understaffed that it could barely keep up with the routine calls of a sunny Sunday afternoon, would have accident reports to write, traffic to direct, and, if things got as bad as the weather people were saying they would, flooded roads to close. On top of all that, there was a county council meeting tonight at which he would have the delightful chore of once more trying to get a bunch of idiots to understand how desperately the police department needed money to hire the officers and purchase the equipment required to keep up with Hargrove's exploding population.

T.J. hated meeting with the county council. "What a bunch of numbskulls," he muttered to himself as he opened the morning paper to the sports section. The Orioles had lost to the Tigers in extra innings. He had stayed awake long enough to see them tie it up in the ninth, then fell asleep with the television still on. He scanned the box score then turned the page and saw that the Maryland Terrapins had started fall football practice. The memory of two-a-day sessions in the August heat made him shake his head. "We must have been crazy to go through torture like that," he said aloud with the hint of a smile betraying him. He had loved every minute of it: loved playing in Byrd Stadium, loved traveling with his teammates down to Tobacco Road and kicking a little Carolina butt. He creased the newspaper open, read the entire article and studied the pictures. One guy, a wide receiver, had more hair on his head than the entire offensive line put together in T.J.'s day. He picked up the spoon, stirred another slow whirlpool into the cooling coffee, and wondered how all that hair could possibly fit into one football helmet.

A hollow voice called his name from under the pile of newspapers. "Go ahead, Helen," T.J. replied, fishing for his scanner.

"Weather for ducks, Chief."

"Looks like it."

"Hate to start your day like this but Mrs. Eaglebutt, the county exec's secretary, just called."

"I believe her name is Eagleton."

"Whatever. Anyway, the exec has issued a couple of marching orders for you to follow at tonight's county council meeting."

T.J. swore softly.

"What was that, Chief?"

"Nothing."

"Order number one: you are to limit your presentation to seven minutes."

"I will not."

"Good man. Order number two: you are *not*—Mrs. Eaglebutt spelled out the word to me for emphasis: N-O-T—you are *not* to repeat the request you made at the last three meetings for hiring more officers. Fat Frank—excuse me, the county executive—does not want you to waste any more of the council's time making requests that you know full well the county cannot afford."

T.J. pushed his chair back from the table and stood up. He cleared his throat.

"Seven minutes?"

"That's what she said."

Rain was now coming down so hard that the roof of T.J.'s one-story house sounded like a drum. He remembered the leak above the den that he had never gotten around to fixing. "I'll give them seven minutes to remember tonight, Helen."

"I know you will. By the way, you also have a message from Emergency Management. Looks like that storm coming up the coast might be the real thing."

Helen Burgess, his secretary, office manager, and self-appointed protector from county politicians and other half-wits, had been with the Hargrove County police department longer than T.J. had been chief. Even though he had to ask her to tuck in her fangs from time to time, he didn't know what he would do without her.

"Ask Jenkins and Lucas to be in my office in about an hour so we can work out some contingencies. Also, call back whoever you talked to at Emergency Management and try to get a handle on what time the storm is supposed to hit here."

"Will do. Don't forget to wear your slicker."

"Yes, ma'am."

T.J. entered the darkened den, trying to remember where the roof leak had been. The room was his cave, his secret hideout, the site of his nightly retreats from the world. It was also the place where he spent many nights sleeping on the worn and sagging couch he had salvaged from his parents' house. Reluctantly, he switched on the overhead fixture and, in an instant, its sharp light dispelled the illusion of a darkened cave and replaced it with the reality of straight walls, sharp corners, and a carpet in whose trampled fibers the simple pattern of his nightly movements had been recorded.

The light also revealed the stain in the ceiling over his desk, cluttered still with things he had meant to get rid of or stick in file boxes—if he could ever remember to bring some home from the station. Stacked next to dusty mementoes of the days when he'd played for Hargrove High School and then at the University of Maryland were the many certificates of appreciation presented to him by civic associations at the kind of functions where he never knew what to say. He studied the location of the ceiling stain, calculated the spot where the water would land, and retrieved from the kitchen the largest pan he owned.

T.J. moved a large framed photograph from the line of fire, studied it for a long minute, and laid it on the stack of unhung certificates. It was a picture taken in a long-ago life that had captured him and a bunch of mud-covered teammates, their helmets raised in obvious victory, as they laughed and shouted words he could almost hear. He remembered who they had played that day: Wake Forest in his senior year. His knee had hurt so much by the fourth quarter that he could hardly stand up, a detail he kept to himself because Wake was on the Maryland thirty-five-yard line and driving. In any game, in any situation, his mindset had always been that he was on the field all alone and that he was the one who had to get the job done. He knew himself well enough to recognize that he still thought that way; whether that was a fault or a blessing he had never decided. T.J. studied the picture, remembering names, hoping they were all well but not knowing because he had never made an effort to stay in touch or go to any of the reunions. He didn't know why. Maybe it was because he had loved those guys so much and wanted to remember them the way they were.

In the kitchen T.J. checked his weapon, holstered it, and pulled on his yellow slicker. Ducking through the rain toward his cruiser, he glanced toward the distant stucco walls of Verna Wilson's grand old house and smiled, thinking about the stubborn independence of the neighbor he had known since he was a boy. Sometimes he wished she still had Major, the biggest German shepherd he had ever seen in his life, to protect her. *Protect her from what?* he asked himself as he slammed the car door against the rain and growing wind. *From herself? From her unshakable belief that there's good in everyone if you look hard enough and that anyone who shows up at her door is welcome to a warm piece of pie and a cup of tea prepared her secret way?* As close as they were to one another, she and T.J. disagreed on that one. If there was even a speck of good in some of the men he had encountered in his long career, T.J. would leave it up to God to find it.

CHAPTER NINE

Water sheeted diagonally across Cattail Creek Road as T.J. turned his cruiser into the wind and headed toward town. He pushed the windshield wiper control all the way up and eased off the accelerator, using intermittent sightings of the painted yellow center line to maintain his course. The woods on his right moaned in protest to the invading wind as the road descended toward the narrow bridge that spanned the creek, a structure that, except for occasional roadway repairs and cosmetic touchups to its truss-like handrails, had remained unchanged since the first vehicle crossed it in 1940. Halfway down the hill, Verna Olsen's mailbox guarded the end of her driveway like a faithful sentry. T.J. glanced at his watch. There wasn't time.

He was almost to the bridge when he decided it would only take a few minutes to check on her. Climbing the long gravel driveway, he drove to the rear of her house where the emergency generator sat like a small spaceship among the ancient boxwoods lining her back porch. It was still there; he didn't know what made him think it wouldn't be. T.J. had insisted that Mrs. Olsen have it installed after Hurricane Isabel, or what was left of it, swept through Maryland the previous fall and knocked out power in most of Hargrove County for the better part of three days. There had not been a power failure since then, not even for an hour, a fact she never let him forget.

Mrs. Olsen opened the door just enough to see who had rung the bell but not enough to let her German Shepherd Major get at the visitor.

"Oh, hello, T.J. Come in. Don't worry about getting the floor wet. It's only water." She put out her hand as though she were helping a small boy cross the threshold.

T.J. laughed quietly but, before he could speak, Verna Olsen held up her hand. "Don't say it. Major has been dead for a year and it's time for me to remember that."

"Two years, Verna."

The old woman shook her head. "Time flies."

The years, for the most part, had been good to Verna Olsen. She still drove the last car Mr. Olsen had bought before he died, a 1990 Plymouth station wagon with a hole in the muffler that made it sound like a tank, a traffic violation that T.J. directed his officers to ignore because Verna had assured him she was going to get it fixed any time now. She made four trips away from the house every week: Tuesdays she had her hair done, Wednesday nights she drove to bingo at the firehouse, Thursday afternoons she went to the grocery store, and on Sunday mornings she attended church, comings and goings that, thanks to her useless muffler, T.J. could monitor from his house on the far side of the trees.

T.J. hugged her, the only woman he could do that to without feeling self-conscious. "If you're not going to get another dog, I wish you would let me put a safety chain on that door for you."

She took his hand, led him into her big kitchen and patted the back of a chair. "Sit down and have a hot cup of tea. Lord knows you'll need it on a day like today."

"I can only stay for a minute. I just wanted to make sure you were all right."

"And why wouldn't I be?" she chided, pouring steaming tea into one of the tulip-decorated cups that had been in her cupboard since the first time the Olsens insisted that T.J. come into the house and eat with them.

He knew her well enough not to argue the point, just as he had learned not to refuse the tablespoon of maple syrup she stirred into his tea, a delight she claimed to have discovered as a young wife who had run out of honey.

"T.J., how old are you?"

That question, he knew from experience, was the overture to her favorite subject.

"Fifty-six."

While Verna shook her head and settled into the chair across the table, T.J. blew away the steam swirling above the maple-laced tea and waited to find out if she was going to approach the subject of his still being unmarried from some new angle.

She did.

"Did you know that Mary Beth Banakowsi's husband died?"

He nodded, awaiting the inevitable.

"Been almost a year."

The tea had cooled enough for T.J. to take a sip. "Verna, that ship sailed a long time ago."

While she studied him, thinking the thought he knew by heart, T.J. drank enough of the tea to be polite and pushed back his chair. "Got to run, Verna. I just stopped by to make sure everything was okay."

"For your information, Mr. Police Chief, I intend to spend the day making banana nut bread for the church bake sale."

T.J. wished she had someone to spend time with, but her only living relative was a sister somewhere in Illinois who, T.J. had learned over the years, was a former Roller Derby queen who now weighed three hundred pounds and owned a bar. T.J. also knew that Verna refused to use the Senior Center because the place was full of old women with nothing better to do than gossip and play mahjong. Walking to the door, he made her promise that she wouldn't go anywhere in her car.

"I promise to stay home, Mr. Police Chief. Now, if you are not going to finish your tea like the good little boy you used to be, why don't you scoot along so I can get busy with my baking."

T.J. turned back before opening the door, still worried about her. Her house was the closest one to the bridge crossing Cattail Creek, a normally sleepy body of water that had nothing but the old dam upstream to keep it that way.

She knew him and his concerns like a book. "There is absolutely nothing to worry about. This old house is twenty feet above that creek. Warren always said the time to start worrying about us getting flooded out is when I see an ark and a bunch of animals on the front lawn. Please let me know if you see anything like that out there when you leave."

He hugged her.

"Who knows, this could be the day that expensive generator you made me buy starts earning its keep."

T.J. couldn't help laughing as she pushed him gently out the door.

Verna Olsen and her late husband Warren had spread their wings over T.J. when he was nine years old. His father had been killed during a robbery at the small drug store he owned, a robbery that netted the recently released convict who shot him a grand total of eighty-three dollars and fifty-five cents. The gunman might as well have killed T.J.'s mother while he was at it, because after that day she lived her life in a trance. It was every-one's belief that, with the passing of time, his mother would recover, that she would start getting dressed in the morning and begin cooking and looking after her children again, but it never happened. She lived the rest of her life walking around in a daze, often asking T.J. what his name was then reacting to his tears with awkward hugs and embarrassed claims that she had only been kidding.

Lured by the sound of Warren Olsen's ancient tractor or the aroma of Verna Olsen's wonderful baked goods, T.J. began wandering through the stand of trees that separated his neighbors' small farm from the property behind his own home. He listened to their laughter and to Mrs. Olsen's nightly warnings that if Mr. Olsen didn't stop puttering around in his shed and come into the house she was going to feed his dinner to the dog. Strapping himself back into the cruiser, T.J. smiled at the memory. The dog they had back in those days was named Sarge, a fierce-looking bulldog that one day spotted T.J. hiding in the trees and came charging after him. T.J.'s panicked retreat ended abruptly when he tripped over a root. He had fully expected to die on the spot, torn to pieces by the wildly snorting dog, not be subjected to a sloppy face-licking, a torture that did not end until a breathless Mrs. Olsen caught up with her dog. The Olsens could not bring his father back to life and they could not awaken his mother from her crippling sorrow but, beginning that day, they made room for T.J. in their childless lives.

The shed behind the Olsens' house became T.J.'s afterschool classroom. He learned about carburetors and fuel pumps and how to gap a sparkplug while watching Mr. Olsen tinker with his beloved Ford tractor and cajole it back to work as though it were an old workhorse. At his wife's urging Warren Olsen promised he would teach T.J. how to drive the tractor the first time he brought home a report card with nothing lower than a B, a promise he kept despite the C+ in art.

The old shed was still there; T.J. glimpsed it in his rearview mirror as he slipped into the cruiser, picturing the tractor sitting exactly where Mr. Olsen had parked it the last day he was well enough to work his field. Neither T.J. nor Mrs. Olsen had disturbed a thing on the workbench or touched the organized rows of tools that hung on the wall above it. Verna had eventually given his clothes and books to the Goodwill and donated his hunting rifle to the annual Hargrove Volunteer Fire Department auction but, as she told T.J. many times, the shed out back was going to remain exactly the way it was until the day she died.

He started the cruiser's engine, drove a few yards down Mrs. Olsen's driveway, and stopped. There was something he had to wipe completely out of his mind before he got back on the road. He knew Wade Banakowski had died. He had thought about going to the wake when he saw the obituary in the paper last fall. Maybe he should have gone but, in the end, he didn't, convincing himself that it would be wrong to come sauntering back into Mary Beth's life at a time like that. He had seen her once or twice since then, one time from a distance at Walmart and another time at St. Joseph's Hospital when he was there to interview the injured witness to an automobile accident. His back had been turned to the hospital room door when she came fussing into the patient's room, demanding to know what the police thought they were doing questioning a man who had undergone major surgery just the night before. In the awkwardness that followed, she had the same startled look on her face and he experienced the same dumb speechlessness as the day the two of them came face-to-face for the first time at Hargrove Middle School.

It had happened; the moment had passed, and that had been that. They had said hello or some words to that effect. Maybe they would have said more if an extremely upset woman had not started screaming for T.J. to get the hell out of her husband's room. Maybe they had said everything there was to say. In any case, much too much time had passed. They were both very different people than they had been all those years ago. *You know that, T.J., and she knows that,* he told himself, *now get your ass in gear and get back to work.*

The flood of rainwater cascading down the road toward Cattail Creek had completely flattened the weeds in the drainage swale at the edge of the pavement, a sight that was merely a detail compared to the volume and intensity of the angry water forcing its way under the aging bridge, a foaming torrent bearing tumbling tree branches and an incredible assortment of man-made junk, much of which slammed against the bridge's rusted upstream guardrail and clung to it like survivors of a shipwreck. For the past five years the county's former public works director, a good man who finally quit in frustration, had done everything in his power to talk the county council into funding the construction of a new bridge over Cattail Creek, one strong enough and high enough to survive what he termed the inevitable failure of the upstream dam, a statement the county executive had compared to the ravings of a lunatic.

T.J. glanced upstream. The dam was less than two miles away, beyond a series of bends where, on quiet Sunday afternoons, he fished for the brown trout drifting like shadows beneath the creek's normally glasslike surface. A question that had never occurred to him before kept T.J. from his focusing on the day that loomed ahead of him: What happens to things like those trout when the creek is transformed into a raging beast like this? Are they swept away with everything else, ending up God-knows-where, if they survive at all? Does some homing sense lead them back to the same still pools again, or . . . The thought went unfinished, bounced from his mind by the sound of Helen's voice on the radio.

"T.J., you just got a call from the warden of a prison in Tennessee. He wants you to call him back as soon as possible."

"Tennessee? Did he say what it was about?"

"He refused to leave a message with a lowly secretary like me."

The heavy morning sky blinked with distant lightning as T.J. left the bridge behind and headed up the long hill toward the center of town. He was able to count to fifty before hearing distant thunder roll across the miles. At almost the same moment, unseen and unheard, another large fieldstone tumbled from the ancient dam into the rising waters of Cattail Creek.

Chapter Ten

In Knoxville, the television station's weather person, a former Miss Tennessee who had donned a red slicker and matching rain hat for the occasion, wrapped up her three-minute description of the most deadly storm in the region's history with a cheerful wink. "Hope y'all can swim. Back to you, Ken."

The anchorman delivered a well-rehearsed ad-lib about his coworker's rain gear before clearing his throat and turning toward the television camera with the *serious news* facial expression he had worked hard to perfect in front of his bathroom mirror. "Without a doubt, one of the most dramatic incidents reported in the path of Hurricane Chester took place at a maximum security prison in the northeast corner of the state where four men were killed by the same devastating lightning strike that masked a daring escape." Doing his best to imitate a mannerism he had observed television news reporters use in larger market areas, the young anchorman paused, raised his eyes from the copy he had just read, tapped the eraser of his pencil thoughtfully on the desk, and announced as dramatically as he could manage, "We now take you live to our exclusive coverage of a press conference taking place at that prison in Mineral City."

The director of the morning news program winced. The footage about to be shown was not live—the press conference had been over for at least an hour—and the coverage was anything but exclusive because every television station in Tennessee had sent crews to the prison. The young anchorman made a lot of mistakes but he was handsome and did well in the weekly viewer polling, especially among the thirty-five to forty-five-year-old women who were so important to the program's sponsors. Reminding himself that favorable ratings like that were all that mattered, the director pointed to the control room.

On cue, a rain-blurred view of the prison appeared on television screens across the state. Beyond an endless expanse of silver fencing, a bulbous water tower contrasted dramatically with the horizontal collection of nondescript brick structures around which the flashing lights of an army of police cars pulsed red and blue. The camera panned to a thoroughly soaked reporter who held a microphone in one hand while attempting to keep his windblown hair in place with the hand that was gripping a wad of hopelessly soaked notes. Doing his best to smile while yelling into the downpour, he announced that the viewing audience was about to be taken inside the prison to join the warden's press conference. He said the warden's name, but the information was obscured by the effect of the wind on his microphone and by the relentless flapping of his raincoat.

The warden, Clayton Vollmer, was wearing a coat and tie but had a military bearing that made it extremely easy to picture him in a uniform. He was late middle aged, square jawed, and obviously extremely angry. His thick fingers tapped the podium impatiently as he listened to a reporter's question.

"As I noted in my opening statement," he interrupted, "the only inmate unaccounted for is a man named Eldon Masters, a convicted felon who goes by the name of Sonny."

Another question was shouted from the crowd of reporters. Warden Vollmer's eyes narrowed to slits. "Since Mr. Masters is the only inmate missing, I believe it is reasonable to assume that he is the one who shot and killed the driver of the van commandeered just outside the prison gates."

The questions were not clearly audible, only the warden's impatient answers.

"As we stated in the press release handed out to every one of you, Sonny Masters was transferred here from the Maryland Department of Corrections. In addition to his conviction for the brutal homicide he perpetrated in Maryland, Mr. Masters has charges pending against him in this state stemming from an earlier assault on three

Tennessee Highway Patrolmen. Obviously, there will be additional charges brought against Mr. Masters if—" he quickly corrected himself "—*when* he is captured."

"Do you have any idea where the escaped prisoner is headed?"

"The state police believe he will have a very difficult time traveling in this storm and may well take shelter in the immediate area until the weather improves." Over the hollered questions of a number of reporters, the warden raised his hand for silence and finished his statement. "To make sure we have touched all bases I have a call in to the police chief of . . ." he pulled a note from his shirt pocket and glanced at it. ". . . the police chief of Hargrove County, Maryland, where Mr. Masters resided at the time of his arrest and conviction."

The next question was inaudible to the viewers but heard clearly by the exhausted warden.

"He was transferred here because of disciplinary issues in the Maryland prison system. My employer, the United Prison Corporation, prides itself on its ability to handle problem prisoners."

Warden Vollmer knew he had made a mistake before the last of those words had left his mouth. Derisive laughter filled the room and, worse, someone yelled out loud that the family of the van driver killed during the escape would be happy to hear how good UPC was at handling problem prisoners.

Warden Vollmer fought hard to stay calm. "A thorough investigation of this incident is already underway," he yelled above the raised voices. "One factor we want to look into is the effect of the storm on today's events. As I noted earlier, power in the prison was lost when the emergency generator was destroyed by the same lightning strike that killed three guards and an employee of a company under contract to the prison."

If he was fishing for understanding he didn't get it. The next questioner wanted to know how a person with Sonny Masters's reputation as a troublemaker had been allowed to leave his cellblock for a work detail. "We have a report that he was assigned a job loading materials onto the very recycling truck he used to crash through the prison gate. Is that true, Warden?"

Warden Vollmer had had enough. His announcement that the press conference was over was met with shouts of protest that almost drowned out the rumble of thunder rolling through the sky above the prison. He couldn't have cared less. His next order of business was to find out who had informed these weaselly reporters that Sonny Masters had been given a job on the recycling crew. He was going to fire the bastard on the spot, and it was going to take every bit of strength he had left to keep from breaking the man's jaw.

CHAPTER ELEVEN

Harold White had lost the argument with his wife and, despite repeated announcements on the radio urging people to stay off the road, they had packed the car and left their home in Cherry Hill, New Jersey, for the long drive to Chattanooga, Tennessee.

"You just don't want to go to Kathleen's wedding, admit it."

"I've got nothing against going to her wedding. I like Kathleen; I just think it's stupid to be out on the road with a hurricane coming up the coast."

He slammed the trunk lid and slid into the car. "You saw those pictures of that mobile home park down in Georgia on the Weather Channel. One of them ended up on top of a bridge a half mile down the road."

"Fiddlesticks! They make up those stories so more people will watch their shows." Arlene White didn't believe that men had landed on the moon, either.

The sky in Cherry Hill was ominously dark on the southern horizon, a fact that Harold pointed out to his wife as they merged onto the Jersey Turnpike.

"Dark clouds or no dark clouds, we're driving to Chattanooga and that's final! This is all about Kathleen. You don't like her and you never did. You don't like anyone on my side of the family."

The truth was that Harold did not especially like his wife's sister Kathleen, a skinny health freak who was getting married for the third time. He shook his head, thinking about the strange array of organic foods that had been featured at her last reception: a collection of arugula, pears, and sausages somehow made out of wheat, an affair he survived by sneaking out to Burger King while Arlene and the rest of the guests were being entertained by a bunch of hippies playing sitars and bongo drums. As far as the rest of his wife's family went, Arlene did have a brother named Bobby he liked. Bobby shared Harold's love of a juicy hamburger and a round of golf and, on the outside chance that the storm would change direction and veer out to sea, Harold had thrown his clubs into the back seat.

"You never even liked my mother," Arlene pouted.

Never had truer words been uttered.

If there was one part of this trip that Harold normally looked forward to it was where Interstate 81 rolled

THE STORM

through the beautiful green hills and pastures of Virginia. Today, he could hardly see both sides of the road through the pelting rain, much less the distant Blue Ridge Mountains. In Harrisonburg he pulled off the highway so they could gas up and use the restrooms. While Arlene did her version of a sprint into the attached convenience store, Harold filled the tank under a wide canopy that was virtually useless against the horizontal rain.

"Which way you headed, Buddy?" the driver of a small U-Haul truck called from the next pump.

"Chattanooga."

"Bad idea," the man yelled through the gusting wind. "I left there this morning and I don't think I got out any too soon."

Arlene returned as the man was replacing his gas cap.

"I was just telling your Old Man that I would get off the road and stay off until this damn thing blows over. Either that, or turn around and head north like I'm doing."

Harold got back into the car, wiped rainwater from his glasses, and looked over at his wife. "What do you think?"

Arlene did not respond as quickly as she normally would and, when she did, it was with a fraction of her usual conviction.

"Kathleen would never forgive me."

As the day wore on, Harold concentrated hard on staying in his lane, fighting the wind with both hands on the steering wheel. As a young man he had been in the Coast Guard, and driving in these conditions reminded him of trying to navigate a boat on a stormy sea. Arlene

77

grew quieter as daylight gave way to a strange premature darkness out of which rumbling trucks materialized like phantoms, showering their car so violently that, until the frantic windshield wipers finally caught up, it seemed like they were driving underwater. By the time the Interstate delivered them into Tennessee Arlene reluctantly admitted that, for once in his life, Harold had been right.

"We should have stayed home."

Harold was too relieved to enjoy his wife's landmark admission that she had made a mistake. "Look for exit 12. I think I saw a billboard for a motel a few miles back," he said without taking his eyes off what he could see of the road.

Sonny Masters eased the Gardner Plumbing and Heating van into one of the long diagonal spaces in the motel parking lot reserved for the growing number of big rigs pulling off the road to wait out the storm. A few minutes later he saw the sedan pull into the parking lot and watched a man hurry inside the office holding a jacket over his head. The car was perfect: dark and nondescript. Starting it without a key would be no problem, Sonny was sure of that. Over the years he had acquired many skills he considered much more valuable than anything his idiot teachers had tried to teach him in school.

To kill time he opened the wallet he had taken from the dead van driver. Seventy-three dollars, much more than he would have expected. He folded the cash, pushed it into the front pocket of his prison pants, and shoved the wallet under the driver's seat. A few minutes later, the man he was waiting for hurried out of the motel office, ducked back into his car, and moved it to one of the units facing the line of trucks. A heavyset woman stumbled toward the door with the grace of a drunken bear while the man pulled two suitcases from the trunk and, as Sonny would soon discover, was so distracted by the driving rain that he neglected to lock the car. After the lights went on inside the unit Sonny forced himself to wait, counted impatiently to one hundred, then did it again. The last thing he needed was for one of those bozos to remember that they had forgotten something and come waddling back outside while he was in the middle of hot-wiring their car. He had already wasted one round of ammunition on the van driver and wasn't interested in using another one until he got to Richmond.

As it turned out, Sonny had no reason to worry. Harold and Arlene White had found a port in the storm and were not about to leave until they saw sunshine again. While rain pounded against their heavily draped window, Arlene figured out how to turn on the television and ran through the channels searching for one of her programs. As soon as she recovered from what she would later describe as a near-death experience on the highway, she intended to telephone her sister Kathleen and explain what had happened. She backtracked with the television remote. Did she really see the words she thought she had just seen: a Meg Ryan Marathon? *Sleepless in Seattle, You've Got Mail,* and *When Harry Met Sally?* She had found television heaven. While Harold settled into the room's one chair and opened one of the golfing magazines he had brought with him, she kicked off her wet shoes and wiggled her wide backside into a stack of pillows. The power went out for a minute, blinked a second time, but came back on just as a commercial ended and one of Arlene's all-time favorite scenes appeared on the television screen. She absolutely adored the little boy in *Sleepless in Seattle,* especially the part where he calls the radio station. While the sound of wind beyond the motel walls rose and fell like giant waves, Arlene and Harold White fell asleep, so relieved to be out of the storm that it would be almost noon the next day before they discovered that their car was missing.

After he got the White's car started Sonny pulled around the motel and stopped in front of the attached restaurant. He didn't want to do anything stupid but he had not had decent coffee since being sent to prison. Staring at the neon Denny's sign through swipes of the windshield wipers, he wondered whether going inside to get a hot cup for the road was worth the risk. As cautious as a fox about to raid a chicken coop, he pulled the dead plumber's jacket securely over the gun in the waistband of his pants and studied the situation. There were only a couple of cars in front of the restaurant; that was a plus. It would take only five minutes to get in and get back out; that was another plus. The deciding factor, the realization that caused him to leave the car and run splashing across the blacktop, was that if anyone got in his way he would blow their damn head off.

Inside, he took one sip of the coffee, and then another, before snapping the plastic lid into place. No more of the brown panther piss he had been drinking for the past two years, not for Sonny Masters. He was out of prison and he was never going back. After he took care of business, it would be like Sonny Masters had vanished from the face of the earth.

As he was leaving, two Tennessee Highway Patrolmen pushed through the door, water rolling in buckets from their rain gear. Sonny's heart jumped. He switched the coffee into his left hand and started to reach for the gun under his jacket before he realized that neither trooper was paying attention to him. One of them was short and stocky and the other was very tall. The tall one was laughing but the short one looked pissed off, a fact that made his partner laugh all the harder. As Sonny passed them the tall one looked at him and stopped laughing. Sonny was a second away from pulling the gun and killing them both when the trooper smiled.

"Gardner Plumbing and Heating, I'll be damned!" he bellowed, recognizing the green jacket Sonny was wearing. "You gotta know Buddy Haskell, my brother-in-law, he works for old man Gardner! Great guy!"

Before Sonny could say anything, the short trooper, who had still not cracked a smile, moved close and put his finger on the stitched name on the front of Sonny's jacket. "Your name Buddy too?"

Sonny had never noticed the name on the front of the jacket but knew instinctively that the worst thing he could do was hesitate.

"Yeah, we got three guys named Buddy. Me, your brother-in-law, and a guy named Barnes." If he had surprised himself by using a name that was constantly on his mind it didn't show. He did his best to smile, an act that did not come easily. If these two cops bought the story, fine. If not, there was always the gun under his jacket.

The restaurant hostess appeared out of nowhere. "You boys better grab a seat and order. We're going to close down in about a half hour so everybody can get home before this storm gets any worse."

The short trooper lost interest in the name on the front of Sonny's jacket and headed for a stool at the counter.

"Say hello to Buddy for me, okay Buddy?" the tall one laughed, following his partner into the restaurant.

Sliding into the stolen car, Sonny spotted the golf bag in the back seat. Because his mind was quick and evil, he smiled. One of the men who had been in prison with him was nicknamed The Golfer. He was doing twenty-five years for second-degree murder, a crime for which he showed absolutely no remorse. In The Golfer's own words, he had killed his brother-in-law for the simple reason that he hated the son of a bitch, and the thing he got the biggest kick out of was that he had done it with one of the bastard's own golf clubs, a putter. *Nice and compact,* he had told Sonny, *the type with one of those mallet heads. Worked like a charm.* Sonny didn't know the first thing about putters, but the one he slid out of the bag had a heavy half-round head on it. Sonny held it by the grip and liked the way it felt. He wasn't going to need any bullets in Richmond after all.

Leaving the motel behind, Sonny bypassed the southbound ramp of Interstate 81 and headed north. From time to time headlights appeared out of the downpour and passed in a blinding shower of water. Sonny was not in a race with anyone; the only thing that mattered to him was reaching the first stop on his list and doing what he had so often dreamed of doing. He stayed in his lane, careful not to drive fast enough or slow enough to attract attention. Windswept leaves, ripped by the wind from roadside trees, flattened against his windshield and remained there until the wind found them again and drove them away. Sonny reached for the coffee and took a long swig. It was no longer hot but it was still a hell of a lot better than anything he had tasted in a long time. Everything was a hell of a lot better than it had been in a long time. Hidden by the storm, feeling smug and totally in control, Sonny Masters worked his way north, his mind focused on the orgy of violence he was about to inflict.

CHAPTER TWELVE

———✦———

Sonny searched above the sun visor then leaned dangerously to his right, hunting for cigarettes in the glove compartment. Finding none, he took another swallow of the cooling coffee. "Coming for you bastards, I'm coming for you!" he yelled aloud, thumping the palm of one hand on the steering wheel. "You thought you had seen the last of Sonny Masters, didn't you?" He laughed like a madman.

Because it was no big deal to him, he had not given another thought to the van driver he had killed. He had killed before and he was about to kill again. All he cared about was getting to Richmond in this weather without running off the road. He twisted the windshield wiper control but found it was already on the maximum setting. From time to time he caught sight of the yellow lane markings that he was steering by, but there was nothing to see in the gray abyss straight in front of him, no red taillights, no highway signs, no headlights on the far side of the highway.

Sonny had killed his father and, years later, he had come back home for the sole purpose of killing the redneck who drove the school bus when he was a kid. As far as he knew, no one had ever found what was left of his father, and the only one who ever even missed him was Sonny's pathetic mother. Someone had obviously discovered Percy Spence's body, most likely when the bowling alley opened the next morning, his car still in the parking lot and his brains splattered all over the windshield. Sonny rarely thought about either of those killings. To his way of thinking they fit neatly into the normal pattern of life: somebody fucks with you, you fuck them back. The killing that had put him in prison was the one he could not stop thinking about. He had not even meant to kill that old fart. The son of a bitch just kept coming at him, screaming for him to leave Sandra and that worthless brat of hers alone. Sonny kept shoving him out of the way but he kept coming, raving like a lunatic about things that made no sense until, finally, he crossed the line, putting his hands on Sonny and ripping the pocket from a beautiful silk shirt that had just come out of the box that morning. Old man or no old man, nobody got away with shit like that.

The whole thing had been Sandra's fault; that was the way Sonny saw it. It drove him crazy when a woman refused to do what she was told to do and, even though Sandra knew that, she had refused to come with him that morning. Ordinarily, she would have been the one he used his fists on, but the old guy was in the wrong place at the wrong time, ranting like he had lost his mind. Sonny hit him as hard as he had ever hit anyone, knocking him down the porch steps backwards. Any man worth his salt would have done the same thing, but in court he had been called a coward, first by the bitch who had caused all the trouble in the first place, then by that two-bit county police chief who stared at Sonny the entire trial like he was a pile of dog shit on the courtroom floor.

The sudden appearance of a shattered tree limb in his headlights seized Sonny's attention. He knew better than to hit the brakes or swerve in driving conditions like these so he held his course, hearing the branch pass under the car, its thumping path between his tires mixing for long seconds with the racket of road water drumming against the vehicle's underbelly. He held his breath, once again waiting for the sickening sound of trouble, but nothing happened.

Relaxing, he felt for the putter on the seat beside him and wrapped his hand around the club's thick grip. This would not be the first time he had clubbed a man to death. His worthless father had paid the price that way, never knowing what hit him when Sonny bashed his head in with a rusted shovel he found in the pile of junk that littered the ground around their trailer. With no more emotion than a hunting rattlesnake, Sonny had followed the staggering drunk into the woods and hit him while he was taking a piss on the edge of an overgrown ravine. He swung the shovel with a lifetime of stored-up hate, knocking his father to his knees then splitting his head like a coconut. Sonny hit him for all the times he had been beaten as a child and hit him for all the nights he had spent shivering with the rats and spiders under the trailer, the only place he felt safe when his father got tired of beating his wife and turned his whiskey-fueled fury on his small son. Sonny hit him for the life they lived, a life that had marked him as trailer trash from the day he started school. When his arms were so tired he could no longer lift them, Sonny rolled his father's limp body down the steep bank into the briars and weeds and threw the bloody shovel after him. In the back woods of Tennessee where Sonny grew up, drunks like his father disappeared all the time. They vanished into the woods or along the narrow winding roads along which they staggered, and no one missed them except for the women they had spent their lives abusing.

Faint flashes of red and blue began to pulse in his rear-view mirror. Sonny watched them grow close enough for the wail of a siren to be heard above the din of the storm. He slipped the handgun from the waist of his still-wet prison pants and placed it carefully between his legs. The police cruiser pulled into the lane on his left and flew by, throwing so much water onto Sonny's windshield that all he could do was hold his course and hope there was no bend in the highway. By the time the windshield cleared the pulsing lights were gone.

He was seventeen years old when he joined the Army and, for a while, there were things he liked about it. It was no small thing to Sonny that he didn't wake up in the morning wondering where his next meal was coming from or that, for the first time in his life, he wore the same clothes that everyone else wore. Maybe the others in his company took having their own bed for granted, but for someone who grew up thinking it was a lucky night when he got to sleep on a moldy couch that stunk of cigarette smoke and his father's unwashed body, it was a new experience. Even some of the Army bullshit was interesting, like being shown how to make a bed with the sheet so tight that a quarter dropped on it would bounce an inch high. As always, when he thought about the way his Army days ended, the anger within him stirred and his strong hands squeezed the steering wheel so tightly that his knuckles turned white.

A big guy named Omar started the trouble by mouthing off in his bullhorn way. "I'm thinking Masters here ain't never had life any better than he has it now."

The others stopped what they were doing.

"You ever notice the way he takes care of that bunk of his like he never seen a bed before?" he bellowed as he fixed his eyes on Sonny. "You ever watched him in the mess hall? He shovels that Army shit into his mouth like he never seen food before."

Some of the men in the bunkroom laughed but not everyone. A few of them saw the way Sonny's muscles tensed like a tiger about to spring and backed away.

"Hey Masters, did you grow up in a pigsty?"

The thing that stung him so much was that everything his tormentor said was true. Before Omar could say another thing Sonny was all over him. He beat the man senseless with his fists then put him in the base hospital with his heavy boots. The Army told him they were doing him a favor by giving him a general discharge instead of a court-martial but, regardless of what they called it, life had just dumped another load of shit on him.

More flashes of red and blue appeared through the rain, this time on the road in front of him. Sonny slowed as the spinning lights grew brighter. As best he could tell there were a number of police cars stopped in the roadway. He had no driver's license but he had a gun between his legs and, if he had to, he would use it. The tunnels his headlights bored through the rain struck what appeared to be an overturned truck, its huge black tires stilled but its taillights burning like ships' lanterns. One of the flashlight beams moving around the wreck separated from the others and moved toward him.

"Bad day to be on the road, sir."

Sonny could barely see the man through the rain blowing through the window.

"Tell me about it. I'm getting off at the next exit to look for a motel."

As Sonny squeezed his legs together to hide the gun

the policeman's flashlight swept over him and probed the car, settling on the putter on the front passenger seat. Sonny sensed the man relaxing.

"Bad day for golf too," he said, laughing. "Next exit is number one forty-three. There are a bunch of motels right off the ramp." The slicker-clad officer pointed into the downpour with his flashlight beam. "Use the left lane to pull around the truck." He tipped his finger to the brim of his hat as Sonny rolled the window back up.

On the far side of the overturned truck, Sonny passed an ambulance and a rescue vehicle whose emergency lights flared garishly before dissolving back into the dark day. Fifteen minutes later he passed a barely-visible exit sign and kept moving, sliding the gun back into the waistband of his pants. All he had to do was keep from running off the road and everything would be okay. Moving north with the storm was perfect. It was almost like being invisible. He swallowed the last of the coffee and leaned forward, doing his best to steer by lane markings that were all but invisible in the sweeping rain. One step at a time, he reminded himself, one step at a time. First stop Richmond then on to Maryland: one old fart who thought he was tough enough to mess with Sonny Masters, a holier-than-thou police chief whose guts Sonny hated as much as he had ever hated anyone, and a woman who still had to learn who was boss. In his carefully worked-out plan, both men were going to die and the woman would wish she were dead every time she looked in the mirror.

CHAPTER THIRTEEN

Rainwater streamed from his yellow slicker onto the already-soaked floor of the Hargrove County police station as T.J. Barnes removed his hat and futilely attempted to shake it dry. As he did so, a creature leapt from one of the four folding chairs crowding the ridiculously under-sized waiting area.

"Chief Barnes, thank heavens you have arrived!"

It was Moon Man, a soaked Grateful Dead tee shirt clinging to his thin body like a second skin. Along with the threadbare jeans and monk-like sandals, it was the only way anyone had ever seen the man dressed. T.J. caught himself in time and used the excited man's actual name. "Mr. Mooney, how in the world did you get here in this weather?"

"Rode my bicycle. I must speak to you immediately. It's about the hurricane."

T.J. put his hand on the man's sopping shoulder. "We

know all about it," he exaggerated. "Does your sister know you are here?"

Moon Man ignored the question. "They landed last night and briefed me before taking off again." He was referring to the aliens who landed regularly in his backyard and left crates of cats on his back porch, incidents he reported to the police approximately once a week.

"Mr. Mooney, you sit back down and I'll have Helen call your sister. I don't want you riding your bike in this weather."

"But they told me you are in grave danger."

T.J. pushed him gently back into the chair. "That does sound important. You stay right here and we'll talk about it as soon as I have time." He squeezed through the overcrowded arrangement of desks and file cabinets to the tiny alcove where Helen Burgess sat glaring at the telephone.

"That was Mrs. Eaglebutt again. You are to call the county executive the second you come in and, in her words, that is an order."

"Too late, I've already been here for sixty seconds."

T.J. took the stack of telephone messages from her outstretched hand. "Call Mr. Mooney's sister and ask her to come and pick him up."

"Should she come in a flying saucer?"

Helen responded to T.J.'s apparent lack of appreciation for her joke by scribbling a note to herself as she followed him into his office. "I'm the one who put that there," she explained when she saw him studying the trashcan sitting on his desk. "It's already half-filled with rainwater."

T.J. glanced up at the stain in the ceiling tile that grew larger with every heavy rain. He muttered a mild profanity and flopped into a swivel chair that, like everything else in the overcrowded station, had seen better days.

"One of those messages is from Emergency Management."

T.J. shuffled through the messages. "Did they say what time the worst of the storm is supposed to hit here?"

"I spoke with a dweezle named Barber. My translation of his scientific gobbledygook is that it should nail us right around midnight."

"Dweezle?"

"Dweezle."

Passing on the opportunity to learn what a dweezle was, T.J. checked the clock above the oversize county map covering the wall across from his desk. It was ten fifteen in the morning. He studied the map, seeing it not as a flat diagram of shapes and colors but as buildings and houses and road intersections crucial to the lives of the thousands of people he and his undermanned staff had sworn to protect.

"Call the fire chief and see when we can meet. I'd rather do it here but I'll go to his place if I have to. Tell him I want to make sure we're on the same page about this thing."

Helen saluted (which, for some reason, she loved to do), spun on her heels, and left to make the call.

Sergeant Jenkins stuck his head in the door. "You want to see me, Chief?"

"Sit down, Mark. We have to talk about this damn storm. Is Lucas here?"

"No sir, not yet. Traffic signal is out at Jefferson and Magruder. He and Suit will be tied up there until the power boys get it straightened out."

The intersection of Jefferson Street and Magruder Avenue had long been the busiest in the county, a distinction solidified when the new mall opened without any lanes being added to the already overburdened crossroads, a cost-savings fiasco the county council attempted to mask by demanding that T.J. assign an officer to direct traffic at the mall entrance every day except Sunday. It never ceased to amaze him that the council and their fearless leader, Fat Frank Reilly, who routinely turned down his requests to fund additional manpower, expected him to pull officers out of a hat to do their bidding. He was spared the aggravation of dwelling on this sore point for more than a few seconds by Moon Man's reappearance.

"Don't ignore their message, Chief Barnes. They are much more intelligent than we are."

Sergeant Jenkins, who like every deputy on the force, knew Moon Man all too well, glanced uncertainly at T.J. before addressing the dripping figure in the doorway.

"What message are you talking about, Mr. Mooney?"

"The aliens. Last night when they dropped off the cats, they informed me that the hurricane was coming to get Chief Barnes."

"Thank you, Mr. Mooney," T.J. interjected, "I promise you I will be very careful. Now go sit down and wait for your sister."

"They were wearing little red helmets this time instead of yellow ones. I think that means something."

"No doubt it does. Thank you very much for the warning."

Cyrus L. Mooney, who held a PhD in physics from Johns Hopkins University, had abandoned a promising career and his young wife in the early seventies to take up life at a hippie commune in Idaho. There, as best as T.J. and his staff could conclude from the background check they ran years ago, he wrecked his mind doing drugs. Ignoring his calls to report tiny silver spacecraft circling above his backyard did no good; he would call back every fifteen minutes until an officer arrived to investigate. Terse reports filed by his staff after these visits stated emphatically that no spacecraft were sighted but failed to explain the appearance of yet another crate of cats on Mr. Mooney's back porch. The appearance of a stocky white-haired man in his office doorway cut short T.J.'s latest contemplation of this strange fact.

"Squeeze in here, Chigger; there's always room for you."

Chigger Mason, the department's radio dispatcher, was a former high school science teacher who embarked on a second career when he realized he could not deal with being retired, a process that had taken all of two weeks. "I hate to bug you, Chief," he said leaning against the door jamb, "but we got a letter from the company that made our radio console."

"I'm amazed they're still in business."

"Funny you should say that. As of November first they will no longer be making parts for our model."

"Didn't you fix it last time with paper clips?"

"Actually, it was picture-hanging wire. That thing is on its last legs."

"Our beloved county executive has been informed of that fact many times, and he will be again tonight."

Helen pushed past Chigger. "Speaking of the devil, Fat Frank is on line one." Following the example of their boss, everyone on T.J.'s staff referred to the Hargrove county executive as Fat Frank, a practice T.J. had done very little to discourage. Helen disappeared from the doorway but immediately reappeared. "Don't forget that there is a prison warden in Tennessee waiting for you to call him."

"I didn't forget. Let's get Fat Frank out of the way first."

Helen saluted.

Sergeant Jenkins seemed lost in thought for a few seconds. "Tennessee, isn't that where they sent Sonny Masters after he caused all that trouble in the prison up here?"

T.J. nodded. "Maybe this guy is calling to tell me he got killed in a prison fight." He stared up at the sagging tile through which rainwater dripped steadily, wondering if the whole ceiling was about to disintegrate. "Guys like Sonny Masters don't usually die of old age."

"What a nice thing for the world that would be," Jenkins stated perfectly seriously as he watched T.J. take a deep breath and pick up the telephone.

"Yes, Frank?"

"It is customary for county employees to address me as Mr. Executive."

Fat Frank Riley, who thought of everyone as an underling, had trouble grasping the fact that, in Hargrove County, the police chief was elected by the voters just like the county executive and council members were. A lesser man than T.J. Barnes might have given in to the temptation to point out to someone as pompous as Fat Frank that, in the last three elections, he had received twice as many votes as any of them. It had never occurred to T.J. to say a thing like that, and it never would. What did occur to him was to push the speaker button so Sergeant Jenkins could get a civics lesson.

"What's on your mind, Frank?"

There was a pause during which T.J. pictured smoke spouting from Fat Frank Riley's surprisingly small ears. Finally, with obvious effort, the fuming executive spoke. "Mrs. Eagleton informed me that your secretary, a Mrs. Burgess, did not seem to take seriously my instructions regarding your role at tonight's county council meeting."

"I can assure you, Mrs. Burgess treated your instructions as seriously as she always does." The corners of T.J.'s mouth hinted at a smile that Jenkins returned in spades.

In an attempt to underscore the authority behind the edict he was about to issue, Fat Frank cleared his throat.

"Take down the following instructions, Chief Barnes."

"I'm ready." T.J. made no attempt to pick up a pen or find a piece of paper.

"You are to limit your presentation tonight to seven minutes. In view of the busy agenda we have to deal with, the time we are allotting you is quite generous."

"Quite."

"You are not to bring up any of the following topics. Are you writing this down?"

Fat Frank interpreted T.J.'s grunt as an affirmation. "Good. You are not to request funding for additional officers or squad cars. Your ceaseless repetition of those particular requests is beginning to annoy the members of the council."

While additional officers and squad cars were at the top of T.J.'s list, the overall needs of his police department extended from a new copy machine to an adequately sized police station without a leaking roof, needs that T.J. enumerated week after week at county council meetings. By modern policing standards, his department's computer system, communications equipment, and training resources were woefully out of date. It had been less than a week since a visiting police chief expressed amazement at the conditions under which T.J. and his staff were expected to work. "The problem is that you've made it look so easy that your politicians think there's nothing to it," the man had remarked as he was leaving. "I don't wish it on you, but what you need is to have something scary happen to this peaceful county of yours, something that would wake up those smug bastards and make them appreciate you."

T.J. had smiled and thanked the man. He didn't want anything that drastic to happen. He just wanted the support he needed to keep things safe for all the decent people who lived in Hargrove County, people like Verna Olsen and all those kids he loved to watch run around like wild colts at Cattail Creek Park. To T.J. Barnes that was what being a police officer was all about: keeping his little piece of the world safe for good people. It might have been a corny way of thinking, but the point of view summed up T.J.'s approach to his job, and to his life, perfectly. It was an observation a psychiatrist or a good wife—if he'd had either—would have made about him a long time ago.

While T.J.'s mind wandered through images of well-equipped police forces he had seen in neighboring counties, Fat Frank raised his voice several octaves. "Did you hear what I just said?"

Once again Fat Frank interpreted T.J.'s grunt as an affirmative.

"Good. Now, one final instruction regarding your appearance at the meeting tonight."

Helen hurried into the office, pointing at the phone and mouthing that the Tennessee warden was on line two. T.J. reached for the blinking button. "Got to run, Frank. See you at the meeting tonight."

Fat Frank exploded in a fit of disbelief and indignation. The last sound T.J. heard before punching the line two button reminded him of a squealing pig.

CHAPTER FOURTEEN

In a clipped, no-nonsense tone, Clayton Vollmer identified himself as warden of the Iron Mountain Maximum Security Facility in Mineral City, Tennessee, and asked for the record if he was speaking with T.J. Barnes, the police chief of Hargrove County, Maryland. Activating the speaker button once again so Sergeant Jenkins could hear the conversation, T.J. replied that he was.

"Our files indicate that you were the arresting officer in the manslaughter case for which Sonny Masters was convicted."

"That's correct." T.J. answered, rotating his swivel chair toward the window as pelting rain tattooed the glass.

"Did he make any threats against you or anyone else involved in his arrest or conviction?"

T.J. slowly turned back around, the storm driven from his mind for the first time all morning. "He did." It was clear that this man Vollmer was getting at something, and T.J. waited for him to spell it out.

There was a long pause that made T.J. all the more apprehensive. "Chief Barnes, the purpose of my call is to inform you that Mr. Masters escaped from custody this morning."

Jenkins, who had been staring at the speaker, leaned slowly forward and stared at T.J. in disbelief. As if anticipating T.J.'s question, the warden added, "Without going into detail, I can assure you there were extenuating circumstances caused by Hurricane Chester that facilitated his escape."

T.J. was not interested in hearing about the extenuating circumstances. "Mr. Vollmer, you asked if Sonny Maters had threatened me. Does that mean you have reason to believe that he is headed our way?"

"I don't think he's going anywhere in this storm, but I see it as my duty to inform you that our interrogation of his cellmate revealed that Mr. Masters stated on a number of occasions that he had several scores he intended to settle back in Maryland when he got out of prison."

As the type of lawman who had too little patience with troublemakers and too much of a tendency to let them know it, T.J. Barnes had chalked up his share of threats over the years. Not counting the ranting of drunks whose courage tended to evaporate as the booze wore off, a listing of the punks, deadbeats, thugs, and losers who had vowed to do him great bodily harm would have filled several legal-size pages. Some of the threats had been delivered in the form of anonymous notes in the mail, one or two of the more original pasted together from newspaper clippings like ransom letters in an old movie. Others had come as muffled phone calls in which disguised voices spelled out in ridiculous detail the fate that awaited him. But, by far, most of the threats had been screamed at his face by livid prisoners being dragged out of the courtroom to serve their sentences. The more dramatic threats alarmed his deputies or, on occasion, caused the county attorney or a judge to pull him aside and urge him, in their words, to "exercise care." But what exactly did that mean? Either he was going to continue being the chief of police of Hargrove County or he wasn't. As far as T.J. was concerned, if any man who threatened him had the guts to do more than just talk, they knew where to find him. He thanked the warden and assured him, as he had assured all the others, that he would take every possible precaution.

"I urge you to do just that, Chief Barnes. This man Sonny Masters has nothing to lose. He has already killed the driver of a van he hijacked just outside the prison gates and will no doubt face the death penalty when he is apprehended."

Jenkins stared at the speaker. "Sounds like our boy Sonny has graduated from beating up women and old men."

"What was that, Chief?"

T.J. changed the subject by asking the warden for a description of the van Sonny had hijacked, a vehicle yet to be found abandoned at a Tennessee motel. He jotted down the information and then, hearing the rain's intensified attack on his office window, asked about the storm.

"I don't envy you or anyone else in its path. If it's anything like what we experienced down here you are going to have your hands full."

Somewhere between Mineral City, Tennessee, and Hargrove, Maryland, hurricane-force winds ripped a tree from its roots and sent it crashing across a grid of power and communication lines. The warden's words became unintelligible before dying into eerie silence. It didn't matter. T.J. had heard what he needed to hear. Sonny Masters was free and, hurricane or no hurricane, if the Sonny T.J. knew was determined to return to Hargrove, that was exactly what he was going to do.

Corporal Suit appeared in the doorway, apparently relieved of his duty directing traffic at the mall. Seeing stacks of files covering every chair except the ones T.J. and Sergeant Jenkins were sitting in, he leaned against the doorframe and hooked his thumbs in his belt. "You wanted to see me, Chief?"

"Need to talk to you and Mark about this storm heading our way." T.J. stared up at the dripping ceiling tile then stood and looked into the half-full wastebasket before sitting back down. "Not to mention the fact that our old friend Sonny Masters escaped from prison down in Tennessee. He killed a man doing it."

Nick Suit narrowed his eyes the way he always did when he was thinking. "You know he will be coming for you, Chief, I don't care what he has to do to get here." He turned toward Sergeant Jenkins. "You remember what it was like trying to drag that son of a bitch out of the courtroom after he heard his sentence. I don't know who he wanted to get at the most, the Chief or that girlfriend who testified against him."

Jenkins remembered. He looked at T.J. "I know a lot of guys have threatened you, Chief, but that bastard Masters meant it. It took the two of us to throw him into the holding cell."

T.J. called through the door for Helen and handed her the note describing the van Sonny had hijacked. "Add to this information the fact that the driver is one Eldon Masters who goes by the name of Sonny. Pull his description out of the file. Since he killed the driver of that van, we have to assume he's armed. Give the information to Chigger when you're done and tell him to distribute it."

Her mouth had opened at the mention of Sonny's name. She looked from Corporal Suit to Sergeant Jenkins and then back at T.J. "Sonny Masters? I thought that animal was in prison down south somewhere."

T.J. shook his head. "Not anymore. He escaped this morning."

Helen made the sign of the cross. "God bless us and save us, after what he did to that poor old man."

"I'd assign you to track him down, Helen, but right now I need you to finish that note and get it to Chigger."

She took one step toward the door before stopping. "Do you remember the terrible things he said he was going to do to you and to that shy little boy's mother when he got out of prison?"

"Helen, the note?"

CHAPTER FIFTEEN

A large green sign materialized out of the rain. Sonny made out the word *Richmond* but the visibility was too poor for him to read the mileage. It didn't matter; he had been to the apartment building where Maury Workman lived many times and would recognize the exit when he got there.

After settling the score with his old school bus driver, Sonny had headed for Richmond, Virginia, where he found a job selling tires and quickly learned that being a salesman was mostly bullshit, an art form at which he excelled. He preyed on pigeons who wandered into the store not knowing their ass from a hole in the ground about automobile tires. He smiled and shook their hands and told the men he could tell they must have played football when they were younger, even if they were dead ringers for the Pillsbury Doughboy. More often than not, they found themselves paying for four new Michelins when a set of basic Goodyear tires was all they really needed, and investing in extended road hazard guarantees that people who lived in countries with paved roads needed like a hole in the head. Sonny made money, good money. Every time he got tired of selling tires and threatened to quit, the owner gave him a raise and upped his commission. He developed a fondness for fine clothes and expensive shoes that made him feel good about himself but did nothing to erase the painful memory of going to school in secondhand clothes picked from a cardboard box in the principal's office.

He met women at work and he met them at bars and, as long as they were good looking and willing to slide between the sheets, it made no difference to him whether they were married or single. His only rule was that he didn't want them to give him any shit. They didn't have to crawl around and whimper like his miserable mother but there could be no doubt about who was boss. If he said, "We're going out tonight," they got ready to go. If he said he liked their hair fixed a certain way, they wore it that way. When he said, "We're eating at your place tonight," they had dinner ready when he got there. There was no stepping out of line. The daughter of the man he was on his way to see was a perfect example of a woman who had trouble understanding those very simple rules. Her name was Susan and she was always testing him. He slapped her around a few times but she still didn't get it. One night, he gave it to her good.

Susan's father went crazy when he arrived at the

hospital and saw what Sonny had done to his daughter. Despite her pleas that he not do anything, her father called the police. The best efforts of two experienced detectives who had seen more battered women than they wanted to remember failed to shake Susan's claim that she had fallen down the stairs in the lobby of her apartment building. She told Sonny what she had done, but he wasn't impressed. He was done with her. She called him; she sent him notes, but he never came to see her. Sonny Masters had no use for a woman who needed an operation on her face and, in any case, he was leaving town. A guy dropping off a load of tires at the store where he worked had told Sonny about a new car dealership in Maryland where he had made a delivery the day before. It was like a damn palace, the guy said, with a parking lot as big as a football field crammed full of cars waiting to be sold. Figuring that the saps who bought cars were no smarter than the saps who bought tires, Sonny left Richmond and the girl who should have listened to him when she had the chance.

Between swipes of the wiper blades Sonny caught sight of his exit and eased down the flooded ramp. It was his intention to hit Susan's father hard and hit him quick, then get back on the road before the storm got any worse. Settling any score sent him sky high, but dealing with the two up in Maryland was what this trip was all about. His heart pounded with anticipation as he slowed at an intersection where the traffic light was swinging wildly on its cables, its tri-colored signals unsure which way to point.

Maury Workman's supply of Diet Coke had run out but his supply of whiskey had not. The window-rattling peals of thunder that sent his cat into hiding caused him to stir in his chair from time to time but failed to wake him. His sleep was so sound that he did not notice when the storm knocked out electrical power in the Richmond area or when his lights came back on several hours later. He was unaware that the daylight outside his apartment window had faded prematurely or that a black-and-white *Cheyenne* rerun had replaced *Laramie* on the unwatched television screen in front of him. None of these things mattered. What did matter was that he was oblivious to the sound of someone testing the apartment's doorknob, a metallic rattling so soft that he might not have noticed it if he were wide awake and stone sober. Maury did stir when the attempts to force the lock became more aggressive, and he awoke with a confused start when Sonny Masters threw his muscular shoulder against the door and crashed into the room.

Sonny closed what was left of the door and smiled at Maury as he walked over to the television and turned up the volume. "We don't want anyone to hear the little party we're going to have, do we?" He swung the golf putter lazily as he spoke.

As thunder erupted in the sky above the apartment building and wind gusts rattled its windows, Maury struggled to focus on the figure standing in front of him. At first he thought he was dreaming. Sonny Masters was in prison. He shook his head and pressed down on the arms of the chair, attempting to rise to his feet. Sonny shoved him in the chest with the putter, pushing him back into the chair. "Where you going, Pop?"

Maury was fully awake now but he still couldn't believe his eyes. It was Sonny Masters. He had never seen the man when he wasn't dressed in expensive clothes, but it was definitely Sonny, soaked to the skin, with rainwater dripping from his dark-blue prison pants and the plumbing company jacket he was wearing. One thing that had not changed was the smug expression on his face that Maury had always hated.

"Your daughter around, Pop? I could use a good piece of ass right about now."

Maury bolted out of the chair, knocking Sonny back into the television. He landed a solid right hand to Sonny's jaw and, with the instincts of an old boxer, threw two quick lefts into Sonny's ribs. Sonny was staggered by the old man's quickness, the same way he had been surprised the time Maury attacked him at the car dealer. Memories of the pain and humiliation he had experienced that long-ago morning exploded with the same mad force that possessed him whenever another human being dared to challenge him. His plan for Maury, devised and mentally executed night after night as he lay awake on his prison bunk, had been to toy with him, to make certain he knew he was going to die, inflicting pain one slow step at a time until he begged for mercy. But now, in his rage, all control left Sonny. He shoved the older man with the strength of a bear. Maury staggered backwards and, as he did, Sonny swung the putter as hard as he could. The sound of the steel club sinking into the side of Maury's head would have been sickening to a normal human being, but, to Sonny, it sounded so good he did it again and again. "Nobody fucks with Sonny Masters!" He screamed the words with each savage swing.

Sonny showered in Maury's bathroom, steaming away the chill that had lingered when he stripped off his rain-soaked clothes. He shaved after changing the worn blade in Maury's razor and searched without success for aftershave lotion or cologne. It was the first time he had stood in front of a glass mirror since he was sent to prison. He took a long look, trying to decide if he had changed much, remembering that Maury's daughter had often told him he looked like a movie star. Susan had been okay, he thought to himself, deciding not to use Maury's toothbrush. Like all women she stepped out of line once in awhile and had to be straightened out, but, until he realized she was never going to be good-looking again, she had been worth the trouble.

He hunted in Maury's closet for something dry to wear but discovered that most of the clothes were too small. He did find a pair of gray sweatpants that must have been baggy on the smaller man but fit Sonny well enough to replace the soggy prison pants. A faded jacket he came across was embroidered with crossed boxing gloves on the left front breast and the words *NAVY BOXING* across the back. Sonny held up the jacket and studied it. "You might have been tough, Old Man, but you weren't tough enough to fuck with Sonny Masters, were you?" He squeezed himself into Maury's bathrobe, threw his underwear and socks into the dryer along with his prison shirt and the dead van driver's jacket, then went into the kitchen to find something to eat.

The lights in the apartment went out following a deafening barrage of thunder that literally shook the building. Sonny stood still in the darkness, watching the lightning show beyond the small kitchen window. He felt great. One down and two to go, and after that he would make sure no one ever found him. No more living in the pigsty hell of prison life, not for Sonny Masters. It felt much too good to shave in front of a real mirror and to take a hot shower by himself. Being alone like this was a feeling too good to be true: no one prodding him, nobody ordering him around. His next stop was Hargrove, the place where he had done it all: made easy money, worn fine clothes, and driven around town with the best-looking woman he had ever met. Like Susan, Sandra Lucas had been a slow learner when it came to understanding who called the shots but, if he had had more time with her, she would have learned. They all did.

Every muscle in Sonny's powerful body tensed as he thought about the way his stay in Hargrove had ended. Sandra Lucas had done what women simply did not do to Sonny Masters: she had turned her back on him. It would have been so damn simple for her to do what he had ordered her to do: look at the jury with those pretty eyes and her big red smile and tell them how that old man had attacked him on her porch for no reason in the world; make them understand that he'd had no choice but to defend himself. Sonny swore out loud, remembering that Sandra might as well have told him to go to hell because between her testimony and the sworn statements of that bastard T.J. Barnes, he was lucky they hadn't locked him up for life. Sonny had relived that trial a thousand times and the only conclusion he ever came to was that Sandra assumed there was nothing for her to worry about because she was never going to see him again. "Well, Baby, guess again," he seethed, rolling his big hands into iron-hard fists, "You and that two-bit cop are in for the biggest surprise of your lives."

When the lights came back on, Sonny pulled open the refrigerator and discovered with a curse that he wasn't exactly in for a feast. He checked the freezer compartment for frozen dinners but there were none. It looked like the man he'd just killed had lived on sliced bologna, mayonnaise, and lettuce. No mustard; none in the refrigerator and none in any of the kitchen cabinets. Even as hungry as he was, the thought of putting mayonnaise on a bologna sandwich was more than Sonny could handle. He fixed two sandwiches, making round stacks of plain bologna on white bread. He didn't like lettuce any more than he liked mayonnaise.

From his seat at the kitchen table Sonny could see the

back of the chair in which Maury's lifeless body slumped. One of the man's hands hung limp, almost touching the carpet. Beyond the chair, the television played to the old man's unseeing eyes. Sonny picked up the second sandwich and carried it toward the television on which a black-and-white cowboy movie was playing. He watched while some guy jumped from a balcony onto the back of a white horse and hauled ass down a dusty street. He didn't know much about cowboy movies. He had grown up without television. His father dragged junk home by the wagonload, dumping it in the weeds on the hillside around their shithole of a trailer, but nothing he dragged home ever worked, not the washing machines, not the dead vacuum cleaners, and not a single one of the dozen or more old television sets. The trailer never even had a radio that worked.

Oblivious to the dozen horsemen who were chasing the cowboy on the white horse, a message crawled across the bottom of the screen:

The National Weather Service has issued a hurricane warning for the entire Middle Atlantic region. Residents in low-lying areas are urged to immediately seek shelter in higher locations. All other residents in the path of Hurricane Chester are urged to remain indoors.

As the end of the message trailed off the left side of the screen, the first words reappeared on the right and restarted a warning that no longer held meaning for the dead man with a putter on his lap where Sonny had tossed it. Maury's dead body meant no more to Sonny than the dirty dishes he was about to leave behind.

A black cat rubbed up against Sonny's leg, startling the hell out of him. He hated cats. A bunch of them had lived in the junk surrounding the trailer his father used to blubber was his castle. His father took shots at the cats for the fun of it but was always too drunk to hit any. One day when he was little, Sonny tried to pet one of them and had half the skin clawed from his hand. He swore at the memory and kicked hard at Maury's cat, sending it across the room like a screeching soccer ball.

When the things in the dryer were done he got dressed and pulled on the still-wet prison shoes. Before he left the apartment he went back into the kitchen and opened drawers until he found the knives. He already had the handgun he had pried from what was left of McNulty's hand when he broke out of prison. He clicked open the magazine and counted the remaining rounds. More than enough to take care of any trouble along the way and put a circle of holes in that asshole Barnes when they met again. Just thinking about that part of his little ramble up the East Coast made him feel good. The last person on his list wasn't going to be shot. She wasn't even going to be killed. But as long as she lived, every time Sandra Lucas looked in a mirror she was going to think about the way she had treated Sonny Masters. He picked up one of the knives and studied it: serrated edge, sharp as a razor. Perfect.

He noticed the cat's bowl in the corner. There was no food in it. Sonny laughed and left it that way.

CHAPTER SIXTEEN

By noon water was ankle-deep in the basement of the old courthouse across the street from the police station, and by midafternoon the Hargrove Parks Department reported that the lake behind the old Cattail Creek dam had risen to the point where the playing fields in the adjacent park were flooding. Baltimore Gas and Electric repair crews were holding their own, but it was only a matter of time before power lines started coming down faster than crews could get to them. With the wind picking up and rain growing more intense by the hour, T.J. told Sergeant Jenkins to have the day shift ready to work through the night and to arrange for the night shift to report three hours early.

To make sure all the players understood their roles, T.J. had grabbed a quick lunch at the Old Line Diner with Jerry Donnelly, the county fire chief, and Duke Cumberland of the Maryland State Police, good men who, he knew from experience, could handle anything thrown at them. At the end of their meeting, lost in thought about the night that lay ahead, T.J. pushed back from the table without finishing his cheeseburger or fries, an event Duke Cumberland proclaimed historic.

Back at the station, after emptying what he estimated was two gallons of water from the wastebasket on his desk, T.J. picked up the phone and carried it over to the rain-blurred window where he dialed the number of the State Office of Emergency Management. While watching cars navigate the rising tide on Farragut Street he asked for Mr. Barber, the fourth player on the disaster preparation team the county had put in place after Tropical Storm Isabel hammered the East Coast the previous September. A woman's throat cleared on the other end of the line.

"There is no *Mister* Barber at this extension. Are you by any chance interested in speaking with *Doctor* Barber?"

Even on sunny days in May T.J. had difficulty dealing with needless bullshit. He turned away from the rain-streaked window and, with an effort that contorted every muscle in his face, managed to reply, "Yes, please. This is Police Chief Barnes."

While he waited, T.J. decided that all he really had to know from *Doctor* Barber was what time the storm was going to be at its worst and how long it would be before conditions in Hargrove County were expected to return to normal. It seemed like a simple question, but apparently he was wrong.

"That depends on exactly what you mean by *normal*."

The words sounded like they had been blown through a very long nose.

"I'm just trying to get an accurate picture of what my staff and I will be dealing with when the full force of this storm hits."

There was a long pause during which T.J. pictured wire-rimmed glasses being removed and examined for smudges. "You are familiar, of course, with the Saffir-Simpson Wind Scale," Doctor Barber began with an unmistakable air of academic superiority. "By inputting this particular storm's projected sustained wind speed into the Wind Scale it can be determined that, in all likelihood, Hurricane Chester will meet the criteria for a Category Three hurricane as it passes through the State of Maryland."

T.J.'s determination to remain patient was sagging like the ceiling tiles above his desk. He breathed deeply and persisted. "So what you are saying is that we can expect dangerous conditions . . ."

"Dangerous indeed!" Doctor Barber exclaimed. "By definition, a Saffir-Simpson rating of Category Three indicates that devastating damage will occur, with even well-built homes incurring major problems such as the loss of roofs. It also means that many trees can be expected to be damaged or uprooted and that power and water could be unavailable for days or even weeks after the storm has passed!"

T.J. imagined the man furiously scribbling his words on a chalkboard as he spoke, pausing to insert a comma here and there, and clapping chalk dust from his hands before continuing. "It would be my advice for you to keep everyone on your staff indoors until tomorrow morning, preferably at a location that is not subject to flooding."

"My staff is the Hargrove County police force."

"Be that as it may."

He thanked Dr. Barber for his advice and hung up wondering, as he had many times before, if there was a proven relationship between high IQs and a total lack of common sense.

By three o'clock in the afternoon the list of cancellations had grown to include after-school activities, evening classes at the community college, and all outpatient appointments at St. Joseph's Hospital. After putting the updated list on T.J.'s desk Helen informed him that the county executive's office had called to confirm that the county council meeting would take place as scheduled but that T.J.'s agenda spot had been shortened to five minutes in order to facilitate an early adjournment. She disappeared for a second before reappearing to add that Moon Man had called to remind T.J. that his life was in danger. "What is that all about?" she asked with genuine concern.

"Helen, it's Moon Man, for God's sake. The poor man thinks spacemen land in his backyard."

"Somebody told me that his IQ is off the charts."

Before T.J. could address the subject of high IQs Helen waved a note at him. "Warden Vollmer called from Tennessee again. He wanted you to know that the van Sonny Masters hijacked was found abandoned on the southbound side of Interstate 81." She skimmed the note with her eyes and read the last sentence. "Subject is apparently heading south and does not appear to represent a danger to you or others in your jurisdiction." She dropped the note on his desk and beamed. "That's a relief!"

T.J. picked up the pink square of paper and read the entire message before wadding it into a tight ball and tossing it into the drumming wastebasket on his desk. Sonny Masters was not heading south. He was heading north with the storm, and anybody who doubted that didn't know the man.

CHAPTER SEVENTEEN

⸺⬤⬤⬤⸺

Every item on the list in front of T.J. had been checked off except the last one: *Attend meeting with county council idiots*. Wondering why normal people never ran for elected office, he glanced up at the saturated ceiling tiles above his desk.

"Helen," he yelled in the general direction of his secretary's desk, "See if you can get somebody in here to take down this ceiling before it collapses!"

"Aye, aye, Captain," came the hollered reply. "Pick up line two before you leave."

T.J.'s finger lingered over the small blinking light. He didn't really have the time, but then again, what was the hurry? He could not remember the last time the council agenda listed him anywhere but dead last.

He punched the button and picked up the phone. "Chief Barnes."

Polly Roebuck, a reporter for the *Hargrove Herald*,

asked if it was true that Sonny Masters had escaped from prison.

"It's true," was T.J.'s careful reply.

"And?"

"And what?" T.J. had learned the hard way to provide the minimum number of words for Polly to recycle into unrecognizable headlines.

"I'm just trying to do my job, Chief," Polly snapped. "The people of Hargrove County are entitled to know if a dangerous killer is heading in their direction."

"The danger heading in the direction of Hargrove County is a monster hurricane named Chester. That is my department's primary focus at this time."

There was a brief silence before Polly replied, "Our readers will be interested to know that their police department can only focus on one problem at a time."

The Sonny Masters trial had been Polly Roebuck's first major assignment after joining the *Herald*, and to say that she had covered the story with a flair for the dramatic was an understatement. Even though Noah Lucas never appeared in court—and despite the fact that Polly's request to interview him was rejected in no uncertain terms by Noah's mother—Polly had elected to describe the killing of seventy-one-year-old Ben Tucker "THROUGH THE EYES OF A FOUR-YEAR-OLD," as the headline above her first report blared. Imagining herself as Noah, she listened to testimony that described Sonny killing Sandra Lucas's boarder as he attempted to prevent Sonny from forcing Sandra to leave her son behind like an abandoned pet and head south with him. Polly feverously scratched notes as T.J. took the stand and testified about the numerous times he and his officers had responded to complaints about Sonny assaulting customers at a bar named the Starlight Lounge, a beer joint Sonny considered his personal stomping grounds. With adjectives and adverbs normally found on the pages of horror stories, Polly painted a vivid picture of a monster named Sonny Masters, the very sound of whose name had caused a terrified Noah Lucas to flee into the woods surrounding his house, where the evils of darkest night were far less terrifying than the man who regarded him as nothing more than a worthless inconvenience.

"Chief, you're not giving me much to work with here. Are you, or are you not, taking steps to protect our community from Sonny Masters?"

When he hesitated, searching for words that would be difficult to twist, Polly said smugly, "I see," and continued firing questions from the copious notes she had worked up before placing the phone call. "You may recall that it took two of your deputies to drag Sonny Masters out of the courtroom and that one of them dislocated his shoulder in the effort."

T.J. pushed back his shirtsleeve and checked his watch. He had to get moving. "Polly, listen to me. The likelihood of Sonny Masters making it up the coast in a storm like this is extremely remote. After the weather clears I fully expect him to be spotted and taken back into custody. More likely than not they'll find him holed up like a half-drowned rat not far from the prison he escaped from down in Tennessee."

He did not believe a word he had just said but saw no reason to fuel a story that would give the citizens of Harwood any more to worry about than they had already.

"And if you are wrong?"

"I've been wrong before, Polly, but right now my department is focused on this storm. If the predictions I'm hearing are anywhere near accurate, Chester is going to give you more than enough to write about." Remembering the unique manner in which Polly had covered the Sonny Masters's trial gave T.J. a thought that made him smile. He struggled to hold back the words but could not resist. "Perhaps you could cover Hurricane Chester from the point of view of a duck."

There was a brief silence followed by an indignant explosion. "What was that?!"

"For goodness' sake, Polly, I'm kidding you."

"How can you be so flippant at a time like this?"

"Sorry."

"You will be a lot sorrier if your duck remark shows up in tomorrow's *Herald*."

There was a silence that T.J. assumed was intended to give him time to reflect on the power of the press. "In the meantime," she resumed, "have you informed Sandra Lucas that the man who threatened to come back and—let me check my notes from the trial for the exact wording— the man who screamed in front of everyone that, 'I'm going to carve up your pretty face up so bad that no man will ever look at you again'—have you informed Sandra Lucas that that beast is on the loose?"

"You can assure your readers that we will do everything in our power to keep Mrs. Lucas and her son safe."

Polly's last question had been a very good one. The day, thanks to endless meetings and phone calls dealing with the storm, had gotten away from him. The truth was he had not yet called Sandra Lucas. He checked his shirt pocket to make sure the note with her phone number was still there.

It seemed much later than eight p.m. when T.J. left the police station. The soft evening light of August had been overwhelmed by the building storm, causing the streetlights to wake up early. Angry gusts of wind buffeted his cruiser and plastered the windshield with rain-soaked leaves as he made the three-block drive to the county office building. His uneasiness about the Sonny Masters situation was much greater than he had admitted to Polly Roebuck. If Sonny had been a rat or a snake that afternoon in the courtroom, T.J. would have shot him dead. The sorry fact was that, as much as T.J. detested the man, Sonny Masters was a prisoner in his charge, and all T.J. had been able to do when Sonny swore he would be back someday was slam the cell door in his face and say quietly, "I'll be waiting."

CHAPTER EIGHTEEN

The council meeting had already begun as T.J. stopped to shake rainwater from his yellow slicker in the marble-floored lobby of the county office building. Muted voices came alive as he pushed open the large paneled doors and made his way down to the front row of the main council chamber where agency heads were expected to sit.

"Nice of you to join us, Chief Barnes," Fat Frank Riley said pointedly, leaning toward his microphone and interrupting a woman in a purple business suit who had been addressing the council members.

T.J. checked his watch, saw that it was eight fifteen, hung his still-dripping slicker over the chair next to him, and took his seat. A glance at the agenda verified that he was the eighth and last speaker.

"Please resume, Miss Melrose." Fat Frank beamed at the attractive young woman he had interrupted. Miss Melrose nodded, squeezed the remote control device she held in her long fingers, and referred to a rendering of the county council chambers that appeared on the sidewall above T.J.'s head. "As I was saying, this is scheme B, a more contemporary approach to color melding than scheme A . . ." and for the next twenty minutes she presented options for the repainting of the council chambers, which, as far as T.J. could tell, did not need painting. At the conclusion of her presentation the council members turned off their microphones and held a huddled discussion, at the end of which Fat Frank Riley beamed once more at Miss Melrose and announced that the council was deadlocked between color scheme A and color scheme C and would take the matter under consideration, meaning, T.J. knew full well, that Fat Frank was afraid to make a decision on such a momentous matter until his wife, Francine, had weighed in. By T.J.'s count, the painting discussion had taken almost a half hour, five times longer than the time he had been allotted to discuss the needs of the police department. He wondered if Polly Roebuck would have any interest in writing a newspaper article about such ridiculous priorities and, while Miss Melrose and her assistant gathered their materials and prepared to leave, T.J. scribbled a note on his copy of the agenda: *Chamber painting versus police needs. What does color fuchsia look like?*

A volley of rumbling thunder rocked the room almost imperceptibly, the way growing waves sway the dining room of a cruise ship, unsettling the water in crystal glasses and causing diners to glance about nervously.

Many in the half-full council chamber glanced upward as the lights in the ornate plaster ceiling blinked twice. An elderly couple conferred anxiously before reaching for their rain gear and hurrying toward the lobby. As T.J. watched them leave he wondered if Fat Frank would display rare good sense and bring the meeting to an early close so everyone could get home before conditions got worse. Unfortunately, the county executive seemed more concerned about his empty water pitcher, tapping it impatiently with his gavel until one of the aides hovering behind his chair grabbed it and disappeared.

Agenda item number two was a presentation by Warren Smallwood, one of the five council members, concerning the urgent need for the entire council and the county executive to spend three days and two nights in Atlantic City attending the annual meeting of the Federation of County Administrators. "This slide," Warren explained in his high-pitched voice, "clearly illustrates that the expenses related to this trip will be returned many times over when cost-savings measures learned at the conference are applied to the county's day-to-day operation." The slide, a morass of red and green lines and numbers, did not remain on the wall long enough for an Albert Einstein to make sense of it.

T.J. could not stand this type of bullshit. It was the kind of lunacy that had driven his decision two years ago to not seek reelection, a decision no one had been able to talk him out of until Sonny Masters killed Ben Tucker on Sandra Lucas's front porch. What he encountered when he arrived at the scene that morning had stayed with him like a wound that refused to heal. Sudden death was hard enough for adults to comprehend, let alone children, but that is what he found Noah Lucas trying to do as the young boy knelt over the lifeless body of the gentle old man who had come into his life so unexpectedly and shown him kindness and understanding he had never before known. Noah was waiting for Ben to wake up—T.J. would always believe that—waiting for him to smile and say that it was all just a joke.

Next to baking, Verna Olsen's favorite pastime was reminding T.J. of his two major faults: being unmarried and fishing on Sundays when he should have been in church. His thoughts on marriage had not been affected one way or another by what he encountered that morning, but the question of his suitability to be a member of some church's congregation had been answered once and for all. Church was not for him. He remembered being told in his Sunday school days that there was no room for hate in the heart of a good person. The words made sense, but they were not words he could live by, because there was hate in his heart that he could never imagine going away. He hated men who preyed on women and children and on people weaker than themselves. It was a passion he did not totally understand but one he made no excuse for. At some point over the years he had grown sick of men who believed that size and strength and the willingness to hurt meant that anything in this world was theirs for the taking and dared anyone to stand in their way.

Dared anyone to stand in their way. That was the part
of their attitude that T.J. locked in on. At his trial Sonny
Masters showed absolutely no remorse. He was livid and
in an absolute state of disbelief that, for the first time in
his life, he had been taken to the ground. The fact that
a woman had defied his demand that she go away with
him and simply leave her young son behind seemed to
be beyond Sonny's comprehension. When the gavel fell,
he went crazy. In graphic and sadistic detail he described
the price Sandra Lucas was going to pay for what she
had done, and T.J., who had heard hundreds of threats
from hundreds of angry men, knew he meant it. They
could lock Sonny up, they could chain him to the bars
of his cell, but somehow, someday, he would return to
Hargrove as angry as the day he left. There was nothing
T.J. wanted more than to be the one standing in Sonny
Masters's way when he showed up.

That meant running for reelection. As much as he
hated doing it, he made the phone calls that had to be
made, he sat still for interviews with reporters like Polly
Roebuck, and he reluctantly accepted invitations to speak
at the Rotary Club, to the Kiwanis, and at the Volunteer
Fire Department's oyster roast, ordeals he looked forward
to the way he looked forward to a root canal. As he had
done the first four times he was elected, he accepted
campaign contributions only from people he knew and
trusted, people who would never ask him for anything
but to do his job the way he had always done it. He had
his sister Beverly keep track of every cent he collected,

and insisted that she return anything that was left over after paying for the lawn signs and bumper stickers and for a crate of miniature footballs with the slogan "T.J. Barnes Tackles Crime" printed on them. The footballs embarrassed him no end but Beverly was convinced that they were a wonderful idea, and she refused to continue as his treasurer unless he let her order them.

And he won. Easily. His sister never stopped kidding him that he owed his reelection to the miniature footballs but she knew, the same as anyone who kept tabs on Hargrove County politics knew, that T.J. Barnes would have been reelected police chief by simply putting his name on the ballot. For nineteen years the big man with the quiet smile had nodded to people at the store and let their kids sit in his patrol car and touch his badge, and they sensed that his being that way had nothing to do with winning elections. They liked the stories they heard about him single-handedly breaking up bar fights and stopping traffic on Jefferson Street so he could pick up an injured squirrel. They didn't know the squirrel had taken a four-stitch bite out of his thumb or about the tetanus shot he had to get after he drove himself to the emergency room at St. Joe's, and they were never going to find out about that kind of thing from him. T.J. spent his days and nights doing his job and never wasted a single minute wondering what people thought of him.

He did have his detractors. The owners of a few bars in the county objected to the way he and his people refused to take the attitude that a little ruckus now and again was natural for hardworking men who needed to blow off steam, an argument T.J. countered by pointing out that many of the brawlers they arrested on a regular basis had not worked for years and by making note of the fact that a number of bystanders, including one waitress, had lost teeth in these friendly dustups. His six most vocal critics were in the chamber tonight, sitting at their custom-made mahogany council table behind polished brass nameplates. Except at election time when all of them did their best to make voters think of them as law-and-order candidates, they tried to outdo each other with jokes about T.J.'s pleas for additional manpower and updated equipment. "Chief Barnes, it sounds like you're expecting Al Capone to pay Hargrove County a visit. Or is it Attila the Hun?" Councilman Hastings Dew had come up with that one at a recent meeting, producing backslapping laughter from his colleagues.

None of them were laughing tonight as they waited impatiently for a woman in a tweed jacket and rubber rain boots to finish herding three excited children to the front of the room and line them up, shortest to tallest, in front of the gallery microphone. T.J. found his copy of the agenda on the floor in a puddle below his dripping slicker. He shook rainwater from it and saw that the elected leaders of Hargrove County were about to hear from the three finalists in the "What Harford County Means to Me" essay contest. Knowing how much Fat Frank Riley hated presentations by school children put a smile on T.J.'s heavy day.

CHAPTER NINETEEN

The second essay finalist was nervously reading from her blue folder when one of Fat Frank's aides handed him a bright-red telephone, its color intended to make it appear that only an extremely grave matter—on par with a Russian missile launch—could divert their elected leader's attention from county business. In fact, it was Fat Frank's wife, Francine.

"Francis, I hope I didn't interrupt anything important."

"Just a bunch of dumb kids reading essays."

"How cute."

"Cute, my ass. Wait until I find out who put these little rats on the agenda." Fat Frank spun in his swivel chair so his wide back was to the audience. "What do you want?"

"Our dinner plans are out the window. The country club closed early because of the storm. I need you to pick up some Chinese food on the way home."

That was fine with Fat Frank. For some reason, he

had always liked to eat Chinese food on rainy nights. He spun back around and reached for his pen, remembering to nod his head gravely as Francine dictated, the way he imagined he would if he were taking a message from the governor. "That's chicken with cashews, mu shu beef with pancakes, and a quart of hot and sour soup," Fat Frank muttered into the phone, adding several more items for good measure. Francine ate like a bear coming out of hibernation.

"And, oh yes, we are completely out of vermouth." As she spoke Francine noticed the frightful storm warning that had begun running across the bottom of the television screen. She started to tell her husband about it but he had already hung up and handed the red phone back to his aide. He added vermouth to the list, beamed at the girl who had just finished reading her essay, and noted with relief that there was only one more contestant to endure.

With its reinforced concrete structure and thick masonry walls, the county office building was arguably the most substantial building in downtown Hargrove. The council chamber itself was nestled in the middle of the building with two floors of offices above it and sizable wings housing various county departments on both sides. Compared to the crumbling pre–World War II police station in which T.J. and his staff worked, the space in which the county council held its weekly meetings was a virtual bomb shelter. These factors made it all the more alarming when what sounded like a train wreck shook the building like an earthquake. The lights went out and stayed out for what seemed like forever before coming back to life and illuminating a sea of nervous faces staring up at a ceiling that had somehow survived the force of such an ungodly blow. T.J.'s handheld radio came alive with the muted sound of Chigger Mason, the dispatcher, calling his name.

"Two things, Chief. I checked with that warden down in Tennessee like you asked me to. No trace of Sonny Masters yet, but he is confident they will find him half-drowned within a stone's throw of the prison when the sun comes up. Sounds like the hurricane barreled through that area like a locomotive."

T.J. watched as the parents and grandparents of the essay readers pulled on raincoats and boots and headed for the exit. Earth-shaking thunder stunned the building again, a warning to all that this was going to be a very long night. He would love to believe what the warden had told Chigger, but he knew it wasn't true. The man did not know Sonny Masters. Sonny was long gone from Tennessee. It was as though the thunder knew that and had raced into town with the wind, sounding the alarm.

"You said there were two things, Chigger."

"Oh, yes; some guy from Emergency Management just called. He insisted I write down his message and read it back to him like I was an idiot or something. 'Chester remains a full-blown Category Three hurricane and is on a track that will take it right through the county, over the Chesapeake Bay, and across the Eastern Shore of Maryland. Major damage and flooding can be expected all along its projected path.' He also said they were closing their office and heading home while they still could."

"The State Office of Emergency Management is closing down during a storm?"

"The man didn't sound like anyone I'd want in a foxhole with me."

"He's not. I've met him. Anything else?"

"Trees and power poles are coming down all over the place. Jenkins called in and said it was hard to tell in the dark but it looked like Cattail Creek was up to the roadway at the bridge out on Baltimore Road." Chigger Mason had known T.J. for a very long time, long enough to give him a piece of advice without being asked. "You're the boss, Chief," he told the man who had to make the final call, "but I'd break up that meeting you're at and tell everybody there to get the hell home."

T.J. pulled on his still-wet slicker as he hurried up to the microphone. He waved his hand to silence the county executive who was in the middle of a tirade about citizens who did not pick up poop after walking their dogs in county parks.

"Excuse me, Fat. That call was from my dispatcher. Weather and road conditions are deteriorating rapidly. I strongly suggest that this meeting be terminated while everyone can still make it home safely."

There were audible gasps from the two lackeys standing behind the county executive's chair and more than a little laughter from the audience. Out of respect for the system or for some vague reason along those lines, county council meetings were the only occasions when T.J. did not address Frank Riley by his well-known nickname. He considered apologizing, but only for a couple of seconds. If he did, Fat Frank would break into his song and dance routine about him being the highest-ranking elected official in Hargrove County and therefore entitled to all the respect that comes with that prestigious office. It was a performance T.J. had witnessed many times before and there was no time to endure it again now. He had to clear the room and send all these people on their way.

"What did you call me!" the county commissioner roared into his microphone.

Between T.J.'s refusal to answer his question and the sight of people getting up and putting on their hats and coats, the county executive went berserk. To the accompaniment of his gavel furiously smashing the council table, Fat Frank screamed, "This meeting is not over! We are only on agenda item number four!"

T.J. worked his way toward the back of the room. "Time to go, folks," he repeated calmly. "The roads are getting bad. Better head home while the traffic lights are still working." When he reached the lobby doors, he turned to see that three of the council members had already left their seats and the other two were looking at each other quizzically. He didn't know if he had the power to close down the building and there was no time to call the county attorney and find out. Fat Frank was now on his feet, waving his gavel at T.J. and yelling something about those who trifle with the power of the county executive. T.J. said goodbye by tapping the brim of his hat. He had to get moving.

CHAPTER TWENTY

⟶⟨∞⟩⟵

Hurricane Chester, born as a restless breeze in the stillness of an African night, had become a monster, screaming out of the sea onto the coast of Florida to plow through the southern United States with the horror of judgment day. Terrified communities in its path hoped and prayed for the storm to let up, or change course, or somehow simply disappear, but God did not seem to be listening.

In the fourteen hours since its destructive force freed Sonny Masters from prison, the storm had roared out of Tennessee, transformed the line between West Virginia and Virginia into an alley of devastation, then veered eastward, setting a course that would skirt the western edge of Washington, D.C., and send it roaring into Maryland with Hargrove County in its crosshairs. Cities, towns, and crossroad hamlets unlucky enough to lie in Chester's path became the subject of stories—amazing, miraculous, and unbelievably tragic—that would be reported on television, written about in newspapers, and retold for generations by those who experienced them.

Tax records for the small coal mining town of Gibbons in southwest Virginia listed a total of 143 houses, one café, a hardware store, and a small grocery store with a single gasoline pump out front. No one disputed the fact that, before Hurricane Chester's arrival, every single one of those structures had a roof. Less than three minutes after a giant oak tree was ripped, roots and all, from a farm field on the south side of town, thirty-five of those houses and the hardware store were open to the sky. While that aspect of the Gibbons story might be told with laughter in the years to come, it would never become easy to speak of the forty-one persons injured by flying wood and glass, one of whom, a six-year-old girl, would die before overwhelmed emergency personnel could navigate the debris-covered road leading to the town. "It sounded like a dern freight train came right down Jackson Street," one resident would tell a television news reporter the next day, "a freight train that shook the glass right out of my parlor window." The body of a retired miner who refused his wife's pleas to abandon his front porch rocking chair would not be found until two weeks later when a pile of rafters and roofing shingles was cleared from the back-yard of a house four doors down the street.

In Louisa County, Virginia, three hundred miles farther north, a small congregation clasped hands inside their clapboard church and prayed for deliverance from the storm they firmly believed to be the work of Satan.

On the wall above them hung a faded photograph of Eldon Sharps, a Confederate soldier who had returned from the Civil War clutching the bible that had stopped a rifle ball and saved his life. Believing this miraculous event to be a sign from God, Eldon had sold his dairy farm and built The Church of Our Shield on a steep hillside high above a meandering branch of the South Anna River. Never before had that tiny waterway been more than a silver ribbon of water sliding quietly across moss-covered stones, pausing just long enough on its lazy trip to the river to form a waist-high pool where, for almost 140 years, a succession of pastors had baptized believers. Brazenly disregarding the earnest prayers of the huddled members of Eldon's weary church, Satan's massive storm ripped through the pines and found them. Splintered wood and mangled bodies blew down the hill to be swallowed in the torrent of muddy water that had transformed the creek bed. In the days and weeks that followed, pieces of ancient doors and window frames and sections of well-worn pews appeared in the mud-soaked briars along the banks of the South Anna and, as the water receded, the bodies of three members of the congregation were discovered among the remains of drowned farm animals. The search for the others would last for weeks and, in one case, for more than two months.

In suburban Richmond, Maury Workman's lifeless body remained slumped in his living room chair, lifeless eyes fixed on an unconcerned television. His cat Buckeye remained hidden until hunger drove it to slink from one hiding place to the next until it reached the empty feed bowl. Two days later, Mr. Gill, the building superintendent, responding to a report of a crying cat, was jolted by the smell of death the second he unlocked Maury's door. Like the van driver whom Sonny Masters killed in Tennessee and like the others Sonny would cross paths with before his own personal storm had run its course, Maury Workman's death would not be counted among the hundreds of deaths officially attributed to Hurricane Chester.

Chapter Twenty-one

———⊶⊷———

T.J. Barnes stood outside the county office building watching the parking lot empty. As he did, the street lights blinked uncertainly, stayed dark for a full minute, then came back on. A large metal trash can, chased by the wind down Emerson Street, vaulted the hedge surrounding the lot and bounced crazily across the pavement, slamming into the side of a minivan whose driver stopped uncertainly before rejoining the exodus. Overhead, a strange light lit the twisting witch-like clouds racing ahead of the thundering storm.

The game was about to begin. That was the strange feeling T.J. had as he waited for the storm and Sonny Masters and whatever else was on its way. It was like being out on the field waiting for the other team to take its best shot. The trash talk was done. "We're coming at you, Number 51! We're going to run right over your ass!" He had heard it all before, just as this time he had heard the weather forecasts and Sonny's threats. He was ready; his team was ready. They knew what to do when the storm hit. Sonny would be his problem. The wind grew stronger and the rain came now in blinding sheets and still, like on those long-ago Saturday afternoons, he was aware of confidence bordering on the irrational.

"Excuse me, Chief Barnes. The county executive would like to see you in his office."

The several inches that one of Fat Frank Riley's aides had opened the lobby door was more than enough for the wind-driven rain to smack him in the face and drench the front of his suit.

"Maybe some other time. I've got my hands full tonight," T.J. shouted back.

The young man looked down at the puddle forming around his polished wingtips. "Mr. Riley said to tell you that's an order."

T.J. shook his head. "Got to go."

"But he is the county executive."

"Unfortunately, we all know that."

The aide wiped his face dry with a handkerchief as he watched T.J. descend the wide granite steps. He had always secretly admired the way Chief Barnes stood up to the county executive and harbored secret thoughts about becoming a police officer. Pulling the door closed, he looked forward to delivering Chief Barnes's answer and watching his boss blow a fuse.

Just as T.J. opened his car door, deafening thunder erupted within a split second of a lightning strike so blinding that the world around him seemed to turn white. After verifying that he was still in one piece, he slipped into the car and was snapping on his seat belt when Chigger called.

"Chief, Franny Kozar from public works just called. There's a problem out at Cattail Park he wants you to look at."

T.J. pulled out onto Emerson Street, wishing his windshield wipers had a higher speed. "Did he say what it is?"

"He's worried about the old dam."

"Shit."

"That's exactly what I said."

T.J. hit his emergency lights. "Call him back and tell him I'm on my way."

Lights still burned in a surprising number of businesses but, judging by the empty parking lots T.J. passed, it was clear that most people were taking the storm warnings seriously and staying home. A posse of Baltimore Gas and Electric trucks lined the curb in front of the Old Line Diner in whose cozy booths their crews drank coffee, ate the best chili in town, and awaited the call that would send them into the fray. On any other night T.J. would have stopped for some coffee and the free commentary that came with every cup, nodding in sympathy as he listened to the owner, Sissy Wagner, make a fuss about the cost of hamburger rolls, or shaking his head with laughter as she described the way Fat Frank Riley's fat butt took up two of her counter stools while he snorted down a three-cheeseburger lunch. Sissy was no lady but she was quite a woman. "Established in 1953," she loved to say aloud, referring to the year her father, Porky Wagner, had opened a hot dog stand on what was then just a two-lane road. Porky's picture hung on the wall of the diner and was featured on the front of the menu, an apron stretched across his Santa Claus belly and his face aglow with a Christmas smile. Sissy was a good person, one of T.J.'s favorites, and at times like this, he felt like he had his arms around her and everyone like her.

He slowed, fought the temptation to pull in, and drove on. Sissy and the diner—the sounds of idle conversation and warm laughter—belonged to normal days and normal nights, and there would be nothing normal about this one. As the diner's neon sign faded into the rain behind him, T.J. pulled into the empty pavement in front of Pep Boys and turned on the overhead light to read the phone number Helen had written down earlier. He didn't expect Sandra Lucas to thank him for the call, but that was beside the point. Sonny Masters was coming, and she had to be told.

CHAPTER TWENTY-TWO

Sandra Lucas woke up on the couch and cursed herself for falling asleep in front of the television. She hated to do that. It made her feel lazy and, for some reason, fat, which she wasn't. From her early teens she'd had the kind of figure that turned heads and gave men ideas, the kind of men and the kind of ideas that had complicated her life more than once and left her with a son but no husband. Not that she wanted a husband. Men were jerks and men were idiots and men had just one thing on their minds. Those were three facts that she had rolled into one unshakable belief, a belief that had been reinforced less than a week before when a very well-off attorney she had been seeing—*seeing*, what an innocent way of putting it, she fumed to herself—had informed her, at the end of a long night in which she had repaid him amply for an expensive dinner and front-row seats at a Billy Joel concert, that he suspected his wife had somehow found out about their relationship and they were going to have to cool it for a while. *Cool it.* Those were the exact words Mr. Pinstripe Suit with the big Mercedes-Benz had used, sounding like a goddamned middle school kid. Incensed at the memory, Sandra pushed herself off the couch and aimed the remote at the television. She was no middle school girl. She knew what he meant by *cool it.* He meant he was done with her. He meant he was afraid of losing the big house and half his money, and afraid of being embarrassed in front of his asshole friends at the country club.

A message was running across the screen beneath a scene from *Pretty Woman,* details about the hurricane that had dominated the news for the past week: *torrential rain, flash flooding, and damaging winds* were the warnings repeated in the endless parade of words. "Enough already," she mumbled aloud. Sandra had heard enough about the storm. Her thumb finally located the right button on the remote and clicked away both the movie and the weather service warning. Sandra didn't like the idea of rain. She didn't like what it did to her hair. She focused on her watch: twenty of ten, too early to go to bed but too late to do her nails. Men were a pain in the ass; she had learned that lesson many times. The problem was that life was boring as hell without them.

On the way to her bedroom Sandra saw a soft rectangle of light spilling through the crack under Noah's door. He always slept with the light on. She had given up trying to convince him that he was safe, that they both were safe. She took off her watch and dropped it into a glass bowl filled with earrings, ignoring their metallic murmur of protest. What made her so goddamned mad was that Mr. Pinstripes had waited until the end of the night to hit her with the news, waited until after he had collected one last bag of goodies. She should have scratched his goddamned eyes out. The phone rang just as she sat down at her dresser and began to brush her hair

"Miss Lucas, this is police chief Barnes."

Speaking of men I can't stand, Sandra thought to herself.

Blinding lightning saturated the Pep Boys parking lot with an unnatural blue-white light, setting off salvos of thunder that shook T.J.'s patrol car. Reminded that there were people waiting for him out at the old dam, he came right to the point. "Miss Lucas, Sonny Masters has escaped from prison and there is good reason to believe he's headed back here."

Sandra studied her image in the mirror and shuddered at the discovery of a wrinkle she had never noticed before. "So what does that have to do with me?"

T.J. bit his tongue. At the very top of the list of things that drove him crazy was the blindness, or reluctance, or self-delusion, or whatever it was that prevented so many women from recognizing that abusive men were human powder kegs. What would it take to wake them up? He still had trouble believing what happened the day he informed Sandra Lucas that Sonny Masters had beaten a woman in Richmond, Virginia, so viciously that she would be disfigured for life. She had not batted an eye. Just days later, that same animal killed a seventy-one-year-old man right in front of her eyes and she still didn't seem to get it. At Sonny's trial she toyed with him like some clueless person poking a stick at a rattlesnake, daring him to make her lie for him. "Go ahead, Sonny, let everyone in the courtroom hear you warn me what will happen if I don't lie about what happened that morning on my front porch! You killed a man half your size and twice your age; you shoved him down the steps and killed him! I hope they lock you up forever!" she yelled at him with a wave of her painted fingertips. "As far as I am concerned, all you are good for is beating up old men and scaring little kids!"

Her words had ignited Sonny. He leapt from his chair and sprinted halfway across the packed courtroom before T.J. tackled him. Sonny fought like a madman, trying to get at Sandra. Even with two deputies holding him down T.J. had struggled to get the cuffs on him. "If it's the last thing I do on earth, I'm going to cut your fucking face to pieces!" He was still screaming at Sandra as they dragged him out the door.

T.J. counted to ten as rain sheeted out of the sky and gusting wind rocked his patrol car. He started to speak then counted to ten again. "Ordinarily I would have a deputy stay there with you until Sonny Masters is back in custody, but with this storm, I can't spare a man." He paused before giving her the message he knew she didn't want to hear. "I need to take you and your boy somewhere Sonny Masters won't find you."

151

"God damn it," Sandra swore softly. She had seen wrinkle cream advertisements in magazines at the hairdresser but had never paid much attention to them. She wondered how long it would be before she started finding gray hair. "I'm not going anywhere," she informed T.J. calmly, leaning closer to the mirror.

T.J. was out of patience. If he had to pick up the two of them and drag them into his car, he was going to deliver Sandra Lucas and her son safely to Verna Olsen's house. He couldn't think of a safer place for them to stay while he was busy dealing with the storm.

The lights in Sandra's townhouse blinked as lightning lit the bedroom windows and shock waves of thunder rattled the jars of makeup and vials of perfume on her dresser. Seconds later, an unearthly sound that might have been the sky being torn apart sent her son Noah running into her bedroom.

"Pack what you and your boy will need for a couple of days and I'll be out there to pick you up as soon as I can."

Sandra felt Noah trembling as deafening wind shook the windows. "I'm staying right here," she insisted, cradling the phone with her shoulder and pulling her son close. "I'm not afraid of Sonny Masters."

Noah stiffened. He looked up at his mother in terror then tore himself free and ran from the room. Bad storms made him nervous, but the sound of Sonny's name absolutely terrified him.

T.J. continued to speak as Sandra studied her appearance in the mirror. "Listen to me carefully. When I get there I'm not going to use the doorbell. I'm going to knock on your door four times. Do you understand that? Do not open your door unless you hear four distinct knocks. Even if you're not worried about what Sonny Masters swore he was going to do to you, please think about the safety of your boy."

Sandra hung up the phone and took one more glance at the mirror before hurrying after Noah.

The dial tone in T.J.'s ear might as well have been a recording saying *Kiss My Ass*. He wanted to grab Sandra Lucas by the shoulders and shake her. Other than that poor disfigured girl in Richmond, who else on the face of this earth had seen more clearly how irrational and explosive Sonny Masters was? What business did a woman who could ignore things like that have being the mother of a vulnerable young boy like Noah? T.J. did his best to check for traffic in the blinding rain before pulling back onto the road. What the hell had she been thinking when she allowed a man like Sonny Masters to enter her young son's life? It had been clear to anyone with half a brain that Noah was petrified of Sonny, as well he should be. One of the points that had come out in the course of Sonny Masters's trial was that, at some point in the course of his relationship with Sandra, Sonny had almost yanked Noah's arm out of his shoulder. What kind of person did things like that? If T.J. had children of his own he would protect them like a bear with cubs, and if he had a wife, he would die before he let anyone harm her. The last thing he would ever admit to anyone—

especially Verna Olsen—was that, the older he got, the more he wished he had both.

The harsh beams of T.J.'s headlights bounced off the wall of rain, creating a glare that magnified the difficulty of seeing the road. *Get to the old dam without running off the road*, he told himself, *see what the problem is out there, pick up Sandra Lucas and her boy, and take them over to Verna Olsen's house for safekeeping until an escaped convict is located and apprehended. Anything else? Oh yes, do all that while the hurricane of a lifetime bears down on the community you have sworn to protect. Just another night in the life of Thomas Jefferson Barnes.* T.J. laughed out loud and told himself if he didn't like it he could always run for county executive.

Some of the intersections T.J. drove through had become angry creeks, forcing him to slow to a crawl. *Take it easy*, he reminded himself more than once, *you are not going to help anybody if you wreck this cruiser.* He was pumped but he was calm; he was confident but, as always, he was realistic. That was not an approach to doing his job that he had learned in some training session; it was a simple truth driven home to him at the scene of a bank robbery one freezing December afternoon during his first months on the police force. A shot fired by the fleeing robber had struck the chrome trim of his cruiser's windshield and sent shards of metal flying. He could have been killed and he could have been blinded, but by pure luck he wasn't. That single shot, fired by a man already wanted by the FBI, had missed his body but changed the direction of his life.

Five agonizing days later, on the front porch of her house, he told Mary Beth Conner that he had decided it would not be right for him to get married and have children. To say he had thought long and hard before he dropped that little bombshell on the girl he'd dated all the way through college did not come close to describing how difficult those five days had been. It had been the right thing to do; he had never stopped telling himself that.

"How can I marry you," he had asked quietly, "when every time I kiss you goodbye might be the last time you ever see me? How can I be a father when every time I leave the house I might never come back?"

She held him tight and began to cry. "Don't do this, T.J. Please don't do this."

But he had. For better or for worse, he had stuck with his decision to spend his life as a police officer, and though he had never been shot at again, he understood clearly that he could have been killed on any one of the thousands of days he had pinned on his badge and holstered his gun. He had lost the only woman he ever loved for the very reason that he did love her, something he doubted Mary Beth would ever understand. A year later, she married Wade Banakowski, a man with a perfectly safe job selling insurance who eventually opened his own agency, fathered her children, and lived with her—happily, T.J. had always hoped—until the sunny

Saturday afternoon he dropped dead grilling burgers on the patio of a big house out on Brown's Farm Road that no police officer could have ever afforded.

It all goes to show you, T.J. thought to himself as he slowed to navigate a sea of muddy water pouring from an overwhelmed drainage ditch. It all goes to show you something, but what the hell it had showed him was something that he had never been able to figure out.

CHAPTER TWENTY-THREE

Though wearied by its devastating assault on the Carolinas and Virginia, Hurricane Chester was still more monstrous than any storm in recorded history as it crossed the Maryland state line. Like a sailor weary of being ashore, the big storm veered east and made for the Atlantic Ocean, seeking to draw new life from the timeless power of the sea. As though incensed by the unfamiliar sensation of exhaustion, the merciless invader hurled lightning bolts at the reeling countryside and unleashed blinding torrents of wind-driven rain into the swollen creeks and rivers feeding the Chesapeake Bay. In Hargrove County, power poles toppled, emergency generators coughed to life, and everyday items became airborne missiles. At a subdivision under construction just south of the town, all thirty-three units were so heavily damaged that they would have to be bulldozed into piles of scrap. On Route 310, four huge plate-glass windows on the south wall of

Phillips Motor Cars imploded, totaling every car in the showroom. A giant gas balloon advertising the dealership's latest sale was never seen again.

At the corner of Maryland Avenue and Hamilton Street the graceful steeple that had crowned Hargrove United Methodist Church since 1928 crashed into the congregation's beautifully planted memorial garden, taking with it half the portico roof. In the course of its nighttime raid, Chester inflicted heavy damage on four churches but on only one barroom, the notorious Starlight Lounge on Telegraph Road. This statistic would, for years to come, remain the justification for belly laughs and clinking beer bottles by those whose decision it had been to drink rather than pray in the face of danger.

As had been the case throughout its short, vicious life, Chester played no favorites. A wealthy man's gated property in the far suburbs was no more sacred to the cruel storm than the Salvation Army shelter downtown on Decatur Street. Rich and poor were struck or spared with the fickle glee of thrown dice. There were tragedies that would change and end lives. In one case, a bicycle left outside in a backyard was seized by the wind and hurled through a family-room window, killing a seventy-three-year-old man who had survived three South Pacific landings during World War II. Miraculously, a fourteen-year-old girl who had run away from home earlier in the day was found the next morning in the middle of the football field at Hargrove High School, almost three miles from her house, unharmed and with no memory of how she got there. These two stories would receive almost as much attention in the national press as an incident on the north side of town in which an eccentric nicknamed Moon Man was seriously injured attempting to rescue what he claimed to be an alien that had become stranded on his roof. Unheralded were the first responders who worked through the night delivering the injured and terrified to Saint Joseph's Memorial Hospital, a sprawling four-story facility that would survive two major lightning strikes.

Overlooked in this perfect confusion was the small dark sedan that arrived with the storm, its single-minded driver undeterred by the wind and rain as he passed the pulsing emergency lights of police units too overwhelmed to take note.

CHAPTER TWENTY-FOUR

—⋙—

"I demand to see Police Chief Barnes!" Fat Frank Riley bellowed as he blew through the police station door, bringing with him enough rainwater to float a toy boat. He had bolted out of the county council chambers the second the meeting was over, oblivious to requests that he pose for pictures with the winner of the "What Harford County Means to Me" essay contest. Nobody called him *Fat*! Nobody! He was the county executive and he demanded to be treated with respect. *Mr. Executive* was the title he preferred, even if nobody but his groveling aides ever called him that. *Mr. Riley* would do, but *Fat*? Police chief or no police chief, nobody called him *Fat*. Not in public. Not at a county council meeting.

Helen Burgess, recognizing the man dripping water on her desk, came a breath away from addressing him by the nickname everyone on the police force had picked up from their boss. "I'm sorry, Mr. Riley, but Chief Barnes is on the road. Between this storm and Sonny Masters escaping from prison, he has his hands full."

"Sonny Masters? Who is Sonny Masters?"

Before she could answer, a light lit up on the switchboard next to her desk. Fat Frank fumed while Helen took the call, smiling into the phone as though she were speaking to someone in person. "I'll call the power company and let them know. Don't let anybody go near it. Okay. You're welcome." The calls were rolling in: power lines in roadways, downed trees, flooded intersections.

"Surely you remember Sonny Masters, Mr. Riley," she answered as though their conversation had not been interrupted, "The man who used to sell cars for Randall Phillips. He killed that nice old man who was renting rooms out at the old Anderson farmhouse."

Fat Frank paid no attention to what she was saying. He gestured at the switchboard, an elaborate but outdated piece of equipment that T.J. had been trying for three years to get the county council to replace. "Call Chief Barnes on that thing and tell him to come back here immediately! You tell him that's a direct order from the county executive!"

"Chief Barnes is on a Code X at the moment and cannot be reached," Helen lied. There was no such thing as Code X, but T.J. had much too much on his plate to waste time with a man she knew he considered an idiot.

The phone rang again. It was Doody Newman, owner of the Shell Station on Carroll Avenue, telling her to ignore the fact that his burglar alarm was going off.

"It must have been the lightning that set it off," he explained apologetically. "I'll cut the damn wires if I have to."

Helen thanked Doody for the call and asked about Mrs. Newman. Fat Frank stomped around in circles. "There are going to be big changes in the way this department is run! You tell Chief Barnes I said that! And you tell him to never call me *Fat* in public again!"

Seeing no indication that Helen was going to hang up anytime soon, he stormed back out into the wind and rain, angrier than ever. He was angry about being called *Fat* at a county council meeting, angry that he still had stops to make at the Chinese restaurant and liquor store, and completely incensed that he, the duly elected county executive of Hargrove County, the third-fastest-growing jurisdiction in the State of Maryland, had been made to stand around in his dripping raincoat while a lowly county employee inquired about somebody named Dee Dee Newman's recent cataract surgery. He was going to do everything in his power to keep T.J. Barnes from being reelected police chief. The next chief would be someone who clearly understood who ran things in Hargrove County. Fat Frank became so fired up imagining life with a puppet police chief that he fantasized parlaying that triumph into the establishment of an old-fashioned political machine in which he would become known to one and all as Boss Riley. The very thought made his chunky toes tingle.

There was only one car in front of the police station when Sonny Masters pulled into the parking lot. Picking a spot opposite the entrance, he switched off his headlights and waited, straining to see the front door through the rain-streaked windshield. Gusting wind rocking the car made no impression on Sonny. The euphoria of freedom had made him oblivious to the weather, to the passing of time and distance, and to hunger and thirst. Before this night was over, a two-bit police chief who had made the mistake of treating him like dog shit on Sunday shoes would be dead, and a woman who had dared to cross Sonny Masters would end up with a face stitched together like a baseball.

Slipping his hands into the pockets of a dead man's jacket, Sonny fondled the solid mass of the handgun and ran his finger across the serrated edge of the knife he had taken from Maury Workman's kitchen drawer. The wait that had lasted the better part of two years was about to come to an end. He restarted the car and drifted slowly across the driveway until he was parked against the curb directly in front of the building. The illuminated glass door of the police station was a little more visible now but not much. He realized there was next to no chance that Lady Luck would deal him another ace and push T.J. Barnes through the door and into his hands but, after the incredible way things had gone so far, it wouldn't hurt to wait a few more minutes and find out.

The sound of heavy rain pounding the car's hood reminded him of sitting in a bowling alley parking lot, waiting to collect a very overdue debt from Percy Spence. The rain that night had been nothing like this, just enough to drum peacefully on the roof of Percy's old Chevrolet while Sonny hid in the back seat like an animal in no particular hurry for its unsuspecting prey to make its final move.

That debt had been even more overdue than this one, the need to collect it growing like a cancer since Sonny was a boy and Percy was the redneck who drove the school bus that picked him up in the morning and dropped him off in the afternoon, stops at which he never failed to pause long enough so every stuck-up kid on the bus could take a good look at the sea of junk and the rusting trailer Sonny wanted no one to see. Day after day Percy spit tobacco juice into an empty Pepsi can and grinned like a jackass into the big rearview mirror while his bus rang with the song his passengers sang until they laughed too hard to sing anymore.

> *Hole in Sonny's shirtsleeve,*
> *Hole in Sonny's shoe,*
> *Smells like a monkey, smells like a zoo.*

The song they made up about him had twelve lines and sixty-four words, and Sonny remembered every one of them: cruel, stinging words they sang day after day and year after year until Sonny grew big enough to kick their cocky asses. During all those years Percy Spence never did a thing but look at Sonny in that mirror, grinning like an idiot. By the third grade Sonny had learned to fight back the tears and take refuge in a childhood fantasy that someday Percy Spence would pay for what he had done, a fantasy that hardened over the years into a violent man's deadly promise.

Without removing his eyes from the police station, Sonny relived every detail of the old school bus driver's last night on earth. He laughed quietly remembering the look on Percy's face when he realized who had pressed a gun against the back of his head. When he begged for his life Sonny told him to sing the song. He told him that if he remembered every word of it his brains might not end up sprayed all over the windshield. The babbling bastard was too terrified to do anything but piss in his pants. It was the last thing he ever did. Remembering how loud that gun sounded in a car with the windows rolled up was as refreshing to Sonny as smoking a cigarette.

Not far from where Sonny was parked, a tree surrendered to the wind and crashed in a leaf-shaking mass into Decatur Street. Sonny glanced in the direction of its muted impact on an unoccupied mail truck. It was time to get moving. Even if T.J. Barnes wasn't inside the police station there would be someone in there who would be more than happy to tell Sonny exactly where to find him. Like a guy he met in prison used to say, the best way to loosen someone's tongue is to stick a gun in their ear. And while they were at it, Sonny thought to himself as he reached for the door handle, they could tell him the best way to get to where Sandra Lucas now lived, an address he had committed to memory and repeated to himself every day to make sure he didn't forget.

The only thing Sonny could figure about that strange business was that Sandra had gotten a big kick out of finding the perfect birthday card, one showing a prisoner in a striped suit biting into a birthday cake and finding a hacksaw blade. *Thought you might need something to keep you busy,* was the printed message inside the card, and *Never knew how good things would be without you* was the way she had signed it in flowery blue ink. Sonny had been livid until he noticed the return address, an unintended piece of information he could picture her cocky ass scribbling on the outside of the envelope while she laughed her fool head off, thinking how mad the card was going to make him. He wasn't surprised to learn that she had moved out of the house where the old man had died, but he was genuinely surprised that a woman as smart as she thought she was had practically drawn him a map to the place where he would find her now. *Big mistake, baby; big mistake!* Sonny had said those words to himself hundreds of times as he dreamed about doing what he was going to do tonight.

He was about to push open the car door when he saw the fat man come out of the police station.

"Hey, Bub," he called through the rain as the man reached the sidewalk.

"Me?"

"Yeah, you. Is the police chief in there?"

Fat Frank didn't like the tone of the voice coming

from the darkened car and, besides that, he was getting soaked to the bone. He started to walk away.

"Hold it, Fat Boy!"

Fat Frank stomped over to the car. "See here! Nobody calls me Fat! It might interest you to know that I am the county executive!"

"I don't give a shit if you're the fucking king of France; I asked you if the police chief is inside that building."

When Fat Frank saw the gun in the man's hand he let loose a volley of prodigious farts, the magnitude of which was lost in the wind. "He's out on a Code X," he managed to answer after several stuttering attempts.

Sonny had no idea what that meant but it didn't make any difference. T.J. Barnes was not inside the station and that was all he had to know. He would take care of Sandra first and then come back. He had all night.

"Get in the car."

"What?"

"Get your fat ass in the car before I put a hole in you."

As he climbed into the car Fat Frank stammered that he had to get to the Chinese restaurant and to the liquor store before they closed. Sonny told him to shut the hell up and listen. In a tone both distinct and menacing, he repeated Sandra's address from memory. "Tell me how to get there."

Fat Frank prided himself on knowing where every street in the county was located. He had campaigned in every neighborhood, handing out bumper stickers and plastic potato chip bag clips with his name emblazoned on them. The latter he considered a stroke of genius by his wife Francine. Remembering how grouchy his wife got when she was hungry, he lied. "I have no idea how to get there. You better get someone else to show you." He farted again, disgusting Sonny.

"Tell me how to get to that address or one of these bullets is going to pop you like a big balloon!"

"Take a right out of the parking lot and go down Jefferson Street to the traffic light," Fat Frank stammered as the cold tip of Sonny's gun touched his ear.

The traffic light at the corner swung wildly in the wind. A few blocks later, when they passed the Chinese restaurant and the liquor store, Fat Frank saw to his relief that both had closed early. At least he would have an excuse for not bringing dinner home.

CHAPTER TWENTY-FIVE

Franny Kozar's public works truck sat on the far side of the main soccer field at Cattail Creek Park, its flashing orange lights blurred by the driving rain and its bright spotlight beam fixed on a point halfway across the lake where a lifeguard chair bobbed like a cork in the wind-whipped water.

"How many times have we told those assholes on the county council they needed to do something about this old dam? How many times, T.J.?" Franny turned away from the wind and let loose with a stream of tobacco juice. "Too fucking late now."

The two of them climbed into the cab of the big truck and strained to see through its furious windshield wipers as Franny worked the spotlight across the length of the dam. Frothing water raced through the narrow tunnel of light, exploded against the rocks, and spilled into the creek below as the ancient structure struggled to contain the swollen lake.

"I could swear that dam was two or three feet higher when I was out here yesterday."

T.J. was about to reply when a splintering crash sounded above the howl of the wind. Franny swung the spotlight to their left and caught the last of a huge tangle of tree limbs sliding down the muddy bank into the lake. He spit tobacco juice into a 7-Eleven coffee cup. "I bet that damn oak tree was a hundred years old."

As they watched, the immense tree crashed into the lake over which its wide branches had spread for generations and flailed wildly at the angry water pulling it toward the dam. Franny spit into the cardboard cup again. "I'll tell you what, T.J., if that old dam fails there will be holy hell to pay downstream."

"That's an understatement," T.J. replied quietly.

His mind raced downstream, visualizing the path of Cattail Creek, banks and bends he had known since he was old enough to put a worm on a fishhook. He had seen the creek get angry after days of rain and seen it rage out of control in the wake of really bad weather, the worst being a tropical storm named Agnes that swept through the county when he was a young patrolman. In that storm, two teenagers had drowned when their homemade raft slammed into the concrete abutments of the Baltimore Road bridge. Without wanting to, he added up the years in his head. Those boys would be grown men by now, was the answer he came up with, and in all probability, have wives and kids of their own. "There is nothing you can do to save people from themselves," that's what his older partner had told him when they were part of the team that came upon the two bloated bodies nine days later. *Maybe so,* he reminded himself as he opened the door of the truck, *but guess who signed up to try.*

"I'm worried about the old bridge on Baltimore Road, Franny. You know how low it is."

"I'll have my guys close it until this thing blows over."

T.J.'s boots sank into the soggy turf of the soccer field as he hurried back to his patrol car. Thinking about the two kids who had drowned during Tropical Storm Agnes had reminded him how important it was to get to Sandra Lucas's house. She wasn't afraid of Sonny Masters; she had made that crystal clear, but it was T.J.'s guess that those boys had been just as sure they could handle anything that life could dish out when they pushed away from the banks of Cattail Creek, hanging on to a bunch of logs bound together with a clothesline. He had known a lot of guys with guts and he had encountered just as many who were crazy, and he still wasn't sure where to draw the line between the two. Right now was not the time to ponder that old question, nor was it the time to wonder whether Sandra Lucas and that young son of hers would be safer clinging to a log in a storm-swollen creek or staying at home unprotected with a man like Sonny Masters on the loose.

The flashing lights atop his car spun alternating arcs of red and blue over the flooded soccer field and across the angry lake as he headed out of the park, thinking, to his mild surprise, how wonderful it would be to see a blue sky again.

CHAPTER TWENTY-SIX

Sandra Lucas sat on a stool at her kitchen counter filing her nails. It was impossible to totally ignore the screaming wind or the frequent explosions of thunder that shook the night, but the uproar had been going on for so long that she had stopped worrying about it. Across the foyer from where she was sitting, Noah was stretched out on the living room floor concentrating on a book about animals. Sandra could see his lips forming letters of the words he didn't know, something he had been doing since he was a small boy. He loved picture books and was so engrossed in this one that, except for raising his eyes when an especially violent gust of wind rattled the windows, he seemed oblivious to the raging weather outside. Like her neighbors, Sandra was unaware that the storm was taxing the structure of her townhouse to its design limit or that her roof was shedding shingles like October leaves.

Noah glanced over at his mother when the lights blinked for the first time, but smiled and returned his attention to the book when all she did was shrug her shoulders. Her son was so different from her, so mild mannered and sensitive, traits she assumed he had inherited from his father—the assistant manager at a bank where Sandra had been a teller, a man she had gone out with exactly two times. *The Loser*—that was the label on the sketchy mental file she retained on him—left for his lunch break the day she told him she was pregnant and never came back. Not even to clean out his desk.

Sandra needed a cigarette and would have smoked one if there had been any in the house. Waiting for that obnoxious police chief to show up was making her nervous. Despite what he had told her, she had not packed any clothes for her or for Noah, and she wasn't going to. They weren't going anywhere with him and, as far as she was concerned, he couldn't make them. The idea of Sonny Masters showing up at her door was ridiculous. Whatever else Sonny was, he was no idiot. Why in the world would he come back to the very place where he had gotten into so much trouble and where so many people would recognize him? She had to admit she had been surprised by the way he had carried on in court that last day, not so much by the way he had sworn that he was going to even the score with T.J. Barnes—Sonny always had trouble dealing with any kind of authority— but by the way he had screamed at her as they dragged him away. Did he really think she was going to sit there in the witness chair and lie for him? Did he and that sleazy lawyer of his think she was some kind of bimbo who was going to perform like a trained seal?

Sandra wondered if there were any cigarettes in one of the many purses in her bedroom closet but fought the temptation to get up and look. She had read an article about yellow teeth in a magazine at the hairdresser that had scared her into quitting.

Sonny's lawyer had been a piece of work, a creep with a comb-over hairdo and pinky ring who had stopped her in the courthouse lobby the day she was scheduled to testify and practically dragged her into a corner over by the stairs. "Here's the deal, Honey," he had started, giving her the urge to slap his weasel-like face, "when I ask you to tell the jury what happened at your house that day, you say, nice and clear, that when Sonny got there he found the old man, Ben Tucker, trying to force you into your house so he could do you-know-what with you. Okay? Then tell how Sonny tried to calm the old man down without any luck and how all he had done then was push the old man away from you and that's when Mr. Tucker fell backwards down the porch steps. Got that?"

It was all a bunch of crap, and she told Mr. Comb-Over that and also told him he could tell Sonny to go to hell if he thought she was going to lie for him in court. The lights blinked, just for a second, and Noah glanced over at her again. She smiled, and he smiled and turned to the next page of his book.

The thing that blew her mind was that, after Sonny

had been sent to prison, the lawyer with the comb-over had had the gall to ask her out on a date. Bowling! He wanted to take her bowling! Men were all rats, all of them. Well, almost all of them. That old man Ben had been an exception. Paid his rent on time. Watched Noah when she was in a pinch, and talked to him about the kinds of things she imagined a grandfather would talk to a boy about. Like in a movie or something, Noah had come to worship him. It was a damn shame what had happened, but it was stupid for Ben to put his hands on Sonny. She could have handled Sonny that day. He had gotten rough with her before and she had handled it. Maybe Ben sensed that Sonny was acting crazier than ever that day, trying to make her go to Tennessee with him and leave Noah behind like a piece of unwanted furniture. Ben had gone crazy himself and grabbed Sonny by the shirt, a beautiful silk one with a little palm tree embroidered on the front pocket that Sonny especially liked. He obviously had no idea that Sonny was extremely particular about his clothes, a nut about them actually, the way they were pressed and the way they fit his muscular body. Sonny had tried to knock Ben's hands away but the old man wouldn't let go; he kept yelling for Sonny to leave Sandra alone until Sonny saw the way the pocket of his shirt had been torn and completely snapped.

If anybody had thought about it fairly they would have decided it was mostly an accident, the old man going down the front porch stairs backwards and hitting his head on the sidewalk with that ugly cracking sound that was hard to forget. But nobody thought about it fairly because nobody liked Sonny and, on top of that, he had gotten into all that trouble down in Tennessee when he took off after killing Ben. Sonny was the strongest man she had ever been around and he simply would not tolerate another man putting his hands on him, state trooper or no state trooper. He just had to work on his temper; that was one of the things she had tried to tell him.

Thinking about Sonny made her remember the birthday card she probably should have never sent. She had found it at the drugstore while she was looking for an engagement card for her manicurist and thought it was a riot. Sonny had never written back, which didn't surprise her much because he had absolutely no sense of humor. She walked over to the kitchen window but couldn't see a thing except three big leaves that were stuck to the outside of the glass like an art project Noah might bring home from school.

The crazy thing about that card was that, even as she wrote the note inside and addressed the envelope, she couldn't decide if she was doing it to be funny or to be mean. She still didn't know what she had been thinking. Possibly it had something to do with the fact that about that time she had been having trouble with a jerk at work who wouldn't leave her alone and found herself wishing that Sonny was still around to knock the guy on his ass, something Sonny was very good at. It was crazy to even think that way, she told herself, easing back onto the stool at the kitchen counter. Why would she want to have anything to do with a man who had expected her to just pack up and leave with him that very morning, like when he snapped his fingers she was supposed to jump, not to mention that he expected her to leave Noah behind with no more concern than if she were putting a cat out the back door.

Noah had finished reading and was standing in front of the couch looking up at the big, framed picture of the giraffe he had spotted one Saturday afternoon at a flea market where she had gone to pick through the costume jewelry. As far as Sandra could tell it was his favorite thing in the house. It wasn't something she would have picked out herself, but she had to admit that she kind of liked it. She did think it was a little unusual because the giraffe wasn't standing around with a bunch of other giraffes in the jungle like the other giraffe pictures she had seen. It was all by itself outside a white house that was mostly hidden by a big tree that was full of what looked like apples. Noah never said much, not even to her, but one day out of the blue, he had gone on and on about how the giraffe didn't care about the apples but had stretched its long neck and put its nose right up against the single upstairs window of the house because it was looking for Ben. Sandra didn't know if it was normal for a boy to say things like that, but she didn't worry about it too much because, sooner or later, he would forget all about Ben and Sonny and everything that had happened. In any case, the leaves of the tree were painted a pretty pale green that went well with the fabric of the living room couch, and the sky above the house was a bright, cloudless blue that she liked.

The doorbell rang, a small sound that seemed to startle Noah more than the booming thunder or the howling wind. The only person it could possibly be on a night like that was that obnoxious police chief. He had said he was going to knock four times but, obviously, he had forgotten. Men were such idiots.

Chapter Twenty-seven

The Willowbrook Forest townhouse development where Sandra Lucas now lived occupied a sweeping tract of land where T.J. had hunted rabbits and squirrels when he was a boy. Its dense stands of oaks and beeches and thickets of holly and blackberry had been home to deer so countless that T.J. often flushed three or four out of hiding without trying, a frustrating experience for a young hunter whose father never let him go into the woods with anything larger than a .22-caliber rifle. "A gun that small would most likely only hurt an animal as big as a deer, T.J. The poor thing would run forever before wearing out and lying down to die someplace where it would never be found. You shoot an animal for the meat; you don't shoot just to kill it."

His father had taught him a lot before dying when T.J. was nine. There is a right way and a wrong way to do everything, was his message, and if you are not going to do it the right way, have enough sense not to do it at all.

That simple message made sense to T.J., and he did his best to live by it. He contented himself with sighting up the deer he spotted and pretending to pull the trigger, his record being six kills between sunup and noon one cold November day when the trees were bare. Fox were cagier, but he came upon them often enough to become curious about their ways. One late afternoon, as the sun retreated into the treetops, he followed a red fox down into a hollow, eager to see what its den looked like. It had taken quite a while before T.J. was able to laugh at the memory of that ill-fated adventure, but he laughed out loud now. Pushing carefully through a tangle of wild blackberries, he had come face-to-face with a full-grown black bear scratching furiously at the bark of a beech tree. T.J. dropped his rifle and ran for his life, terrified more by the monster-like enormity of the bear's head than by the powerful curved claws shredding the trunk of the tree. His father had believed his story, every word of it. The woods in this part of Hargrove County had been full of bear when he himself was a boy, he had said, settling into the worn chair next to the fireplace where he spent winter evenings. "But bear or no bear, you get back out there first thing in the morning and find that rifle." There was a right way and a wrong way to do everything.

Except for sparse gatherings of naked trees between the clustered townhouses, those magical woods of his childhood were now gone, bulldozed like so much land in the county to make way for real estate developments the county council approved with far less scrutiny than they aimed at many other items on their agenda, items like T.J.'s own requests for funds to properly protect the county they were allowing to mushroom. The hell with them, he swore to himself as he slowed to turn off the highway, when this term was up the voters of Hargrove County were going to have to find somebody else willing to waste time being jerked around by that bunch of idiots on the county council. T.J. would be the first one to admit he had made that vow before, but this time nothing on earth was going to make him change his mind.

Ponded water pounded the underside of his cruiser, snapping T.J. back to reality. The entrance to Willowbrook Forest was already flooded hubcap-high, and it was only a matter of time before runoff from asphalt driveways and parking areas within the rabbit warren of townhouses made the entrance impassable. There was not going to be time for T.J. to get into a debate with Sandra Lucas over the pros and cons of taking her and her young son somewhere they would be safe. They were coming with him and they were staying where he took them until, one way or another, Sonny Masters was no longer a threat to them or anyone else. T.J.'s spotlight swept the numbers of the units until he found the one he was searching for. Pulling up the zipper of his slicker, he dove into the storm, ducked through a waterfall of rainwater cascading from an overwhelmed gutter atop Sandra Lucas's porch, and pounded on her door. Four times; four distinct knocks; no more, no less; that was what he had told her. A flash of

blinding lightning ignited a barrage of thunder so shat-
tering that the rain seemed to stop for a second in awed
response. High above the small concrete porch, a soaring
willow oak reeled wildly in the unrelenting gusts, its long
naked trunk left vulnerable when the builder cleared
the thick woods protecting it. "Come on, God damn it,"
T.J. swore unheard, "I'm standing under Niagara Falls
out here!" The sound of angry voices erupted inside the
townhouse, but before he could process this information
the door opened just enough for him to recognize Sandra
Lucas. She was wearing a sweatshirt and jeans. Her nose
was bleeding, and the left side of her face was purple and
swollen. Instantly, the angry voices T.J. had heard made
sense. He reached through the slit in his rain slicker, but
before his gun cleared its holster, Sandra Lucas was yanked
backwards by her hair and the door flew wide open.

"What a nice surprise!" Sonny Masters bellowed into
the wind and rain. "Hands where I can see them!"

Sonny waved him into the foyer. The gun in his
hand was a .40-caliber model commonly used by law
enforcement officers and identical to one T.J. had once
confiscated from a teenager who used it to fire at the
house of a neighbor who had refused to return a soccer
ball accidentally kicked into his yard. That highly illegal
act of retaliation had split a brick at the top of the man's
chimney, a nugget of knowledge T.J. did his best not to
dwell on. Sonny slammed the door against the raging
storm, shutting out the windblown rain that had swept
across the white tile floor.

"If it isn't my favorite cop. I thought I was going to have to go looking for you after I got done taking care of Fat Boy over there."

T.J. followed Sonny's eyes into the living room where, to his astonishment, a shaking Fat Frank Riley slumped on the couch, weeping like a baby, his puffy face moon pale. Drying blood matted his sparse wet hair and streaked the left side of his face. The lamp in the living room went dark, stayed that way for long seconds, then lit again as the full might of Hurricane Chester found the defenseless townhouses and shook them to their foundations.

"Arrest that man!" Fat Frank screamed, struggling to hoist himself to his feet. "You're the police chief! That's what we pay you for!"

Before T.J. could even begin to make sense of the county executive's presence in Sandra Lucas's town-house, Sonny's gun erupted, blowing a hole in the wall over Fat Frank's head. "Sit down, Fat Boy, or I'll kill you right now!"

"Don't shoot me!" Frank Riley screamed, crossing his beefy arms in front of his face and slumping back onto the couch. "Let me go and I won't tell a soul about any of this! I swear to God, I won't!" His sobbing degenerated into quick pig-like snorts. "You have to let me go. My wife is waiting for me to bring home Chinese food and vermouth. She'll call the police. They'll come looking for me."

"The police are already here, asshole," Sonny sneered, returning his attention to T.J. "Open that rain gear real

183

slow and hand me your gun. Do anything smart and I'll put a couple of slugs in your balls."

T.J. did what he was told, glancing at Sandra Lucas, who was leaning on the kitchen counter, glaring at Sonny. Even in old jeans and a faded Ocean City sweatshirt, she was a good-looking woman. No matter what else T.J. thought of her, he had to give her that.

"Where is your boy, Miss Lucas?" T.J. asked.

"He ran out the kitchen door the second he heard Sonny's voice. I tried to go after him but this jerk wouldn't let me." Her eyes never left Sonny as she spoke. "Noah still has nightmares about the day Sonny killed that poor old man on our front porch."

"That old fart asked for it, putting his hands on me the way he did!"

"He was trying to protect us, Sonny! From you!"

A good cop wasn't supposed to hate anyone—it got in the way of doing a tough job the right way—but every time T.J. thought about Sandra Lucas's young son kneeling in stunned horror beside the lifeless body of the quiet old man who had befriended him, an emotion as close to hate as T.J. had ever experienced threatened to affect his judgment. He wanted desperately to do something, anything, but a man with no more feelings than a snake was pointing a powerful handgun at his belly. T.J. wouldn't make it two steps in Sonny's direction, and after that the others would have no one on their side.

"Noah's going to get hurt, Sonny," Sandra pleaded. "Listen to that storm! He doesn't even have shoes on, much less a jacket! Don't you care about that?"

It was a stupid question, and she knew the answer better than anyone. Sonny didn't give a damn about Noah. He didn't give a damn about her. He didn't give a damn about anyone but himself. Remembering that she once thought she could change all that made her so damn mad she wanted to scream.

As though he had read her mind, Sonny grinned. He stuck the prison guard's gun into the pocket of his soaked jacket and, fondling T.J.'s handgun like a new toy, pushed Sandra toward the kitchen door. "Open it! Go ahead! Open it! Maybe the little bastard will come back in."

Sandra seemed confused but pulled the door open. The second she did, Sonny shoved her aside and fired four thunderous shots into the blinding gale. "If that doesn't take care of the little bastard maybe the lightning will!"

"Sonny!" T.J. lunged for Sonny, who spun around and shoved the gun in his face.

"Now turn around."

When he did, T.J.'s head exploded in a burst of stars. He didn't lose consciousness, at least he didn't think he did, but when his head began to clear, he found himself on the floor in the living room, staring at Fat Frank's stubby, rain-soaked shoes.

"Don't pass out, Copper," Sonny hissed in his ear. "I want you to know you're going to die. I want you to lie there and think about that scary little fact. Remember the way you looked at me in the courtroom like I was a pile of dog shit? Think about that for a few minutes and then think about the way your brain is going to be splattered all over the floor when I get done squeezing this trigger."

The townhouse lights flickered as thunder rolled through the sky like a low-flying bomber.

"Don't shoot me!" Fat Frank wailed. "Shoot him, but please don't shoot me! Let me go and I'll tell everybody you treated me well. I'll tell them anything you want me to. I'm the county executive, they'll believe me."

"You pathetic bastard!" Sonny's gun roared twice. Frank Riley gasped as he tried to rise from the couch, his big arms reaching for something that wasn't there. The lights flickered again and somewhere upstairs a window swung open in an explosion of crashing glass. The huge man slumped forward and collapsed on top of T.J. like a dead elephant. A second later, the lights went out again as rain drummed against the side of the townhouse and wind rattled the windows, masking T.J.'s struggle to catch his breath.

"Sonny!" Sandra screamed. "You worthless animal!"

Above the roar of the storm T.J. heard sounds of a struggle. Sandra continued to scream at Sonny until a sharp smack quieted her. "I'm going to kill that fucking cop and then it's going to be just you and me!"

The storm seemed to be passing directly over them. Thunder shook the floor beneath T.J. and sent a grotesque shudder through Fat Frank Riley's lifeless body. Lightning flashed beyond the drapery-covered windows, illuminating the room in crazy patterns of light before the townhouse went black and stayed black.

A second later, T.J. heard a door open and felt the tremendous force of the storm sweep inside. Dishes and lamps crashed to the floor as a blast of rainwater drenched T.J.'s right arm and hand, the only parts of his body not fully protected by Fat Frank's body.

"Get back in here you bitch!" Sonny screamed at the top of his lungs.

For long minutes the only sounds that T.J. heard were the violent cries of the storm. His best guess was that Sandra had made a run for it and Sonny had gone after her. There was no doubt in his mind that he was next on Sonny's execution list but, for some reason, that thought didn't scare him. In his more than thirty years on the police force T.J. Barnes had been shot at one time and been able to return fire, hitting the man square in the chest and killing him. Other than at the practice range, he had not fired his service weapon since. He didn't feel good about what he had done that day at the bank, and he didn't feel bad about it. Mainly, he felt happy to be alive. He had done what he had been trained to do and he knew he could do it again.

This time T.J. had no gun and there was going to be no police car between him and the man he knew was going to come back to kill him. His only protection was the enormous lifeless body that was squeezing the breath out of him and the sea of darkness that could vanish and betray him with the next surge of electricity.

Outside, Sonny had caught up with Sandra before she reached the corner of her building. She was shouting at the top of her lungs for Noah, shouts that were swept away with the sea of wildly swirling leaves. Sonny grabbed her rain-matted hair and dragged her back toward the open townhouse door. "You're coming with me this time, God damn it, and when I get done with you the sight of your face is going to make people sick!"

"I'll go with you!" she screamed against the roar of the storm. "Let me find Noah and I'll go with you!"

"The hell with the little bastard! Let him drown!"

"Sonny!" She swung at him, hitting him in the face, and he hit her back with the hand grasping T.J.'s gun. Her knees buckled, making it harder for him to pull her up the overflowing stairs to her townhouse. She struggled against him with all her strength but it did no good; Sonny, in his fury, was unstoppable.

"I didn't come all this way to leave without killing that fucking cop!"

Chapter Twenty-eight

Inside, under the enormous weight of Fat Frank Riley's massive body, T.J. was having trouble breathing. He had managed to free one arm and twist his aching head until he was able see lightning strikes set the living room windows on fire. Between these blinding displays there were only the sounds of the storm: the front door slamming relentlessly on its hinges, wildly rattling window panes, and, as though the townhouse itself were alive, the strange, deep moaning of a structure on the verge of surrendering to forces it had never been intended to resist.

Outside, Sonny, half-blinded by the rain, yanked Sandra up to the front door and did his best to hold her still while he searched the darkness for his target. Even with her twisting body and flailing arms interfering with his ability to hone in on the spot where he had left T.J. lying on the floor, he resisted the temptation to shoot her dead. It had been almost two years since he had been with a woman and, as livid as he was about the way she had treated him, he wasn't about to put a bullet into her sexy body. He slammed her in the face with the side of the handgun and experienced a rush of satisfaction as she cried out and slumped onto the porch. She had never understood that he was the boss; she had refused to help him at the trial; and, on top of everything else, she had sent him a smart-ass birthday card while he was locked up like an animal, smug in her belief that she would never see him again. Sonny was going to have one last round of fun with her and then perform a little kitchen-knife surgery on her pretty face. Everyone on his list was going to pay the price for fucking with Sonny Masters. A tremendous blast of lightning lit the interior of the town-house, illuminating for a split second the shape of a body on the floor in front of the couch. Sonny fired repeatedly into the cave-black living room, emptying his gun in the direction of a target he was sure he could not miss.

The first three shots slammed into the dead man's body so violently that T.J. felt their sickening vibrations. The roar of the fourth one jolted T.J.'s head as searing pain screamed through his left ear. The final two, affected as much by the wind and the rain as by Sandra's renewed attempts to break free from Sonny, rocked the living room wall with such force that the large framed picture above the couch crashed to the floor. As if Sonny's shots had angered the storm, the wind renewed its assault on the overmatched willow oak in the front yard and sent it crashing onto the building. Roofing, rafters, joists, and plywood splintered into piles of debris. Once again the shield that was Fat Frank's huge body saved T.J.'s life, a bizarre fact that he would never forget. Sonny fired his gun irrationally into the remains of a still-quivering mass of branches that had narrowly missed him. He cursed the hollow click of an empty chamber and hurled T.J.'s gun into the night. There was no doubt in his mind that, if some of the spent shots had not killed the hated cop, the huge crashing tree had. Laughing like a madman at the thought that T.J. Barnes had been hit by shots from his own gun, Sonny dragged Sandra through the driving rain to his car.

Crawling, pushing, and swearing, T.J. freed himself from the suffocating weight of Frank Riley's body and knelt on one knee until he was strong enough to stand. His shredded ear throbbed in time with his racing heart as warm blood slid down the side of his face, soaking the collar of his shirt. His gold standard for pain had always been the compound thumb fracture he had suffered in a game against Georgia Tech. If that injury had been a ten, the stinging pain in his ear was maybe an eight, no way near bad enough to keep him from doing what he had to do. Lightning lit the room for a few stuttering seconds, illuminating Fat Frank's massive remains. The sobering realization that he had never liked the man wrapped T.J.'s physical pain with guilt. He had never done a damn thing to stop himself or the people who worked for him from referring to the county executive by the nickname the man hated. If anything, his own attitude had encouraged their jokes. Pulsing lightning once again illuminated the huge corpse like a scene from a horror movie. With the force of an odd, earthly prayer, T.J. swore that no one would ever hear from him that Frank Riley had cried like a baby and begged for his life. That was the least he could do. It was undoubtedly the last thing on the man's mind, but Frank Riley had saved T.J.'s life.

T.J. made the sign of the cross for the first time since grade school and began picking his way through the debris of the wrecked townhouse toward the sound of a door being ripped from its hinges in the raging storm. Fat—T.J. caught himself—Frank Riley had a wife, an excitable woman almost as overweight as her husband, whom T.J. had come to know while enduring the civic functions he detested. Somebody would have to tell her. Somebody would have to make their way here and remove Frank's body. T.J. would call for help from the road, but he could not wait around for it to arrive. His hands were full. Sonny Masters, the man who killed the Hargrove County executive with no more emotion than swatting a fly, had disappeared into the storm with Sandra Lucas, and it would only be a matter of time before he found someplace to pull over and do to her what he come a long way to do.

CHAPTER TWENTY-NINE

Pushing a tree branch from the roof of his cruiser, T.J. climbed in, bringing a bucket of rainwater with him. The second he switched on his headlights he saw the boy running toward him.

"Noah, good God! I forgot all about you!" "

T.J. picked him up, lifted him into the car, and clicked the seatbelt closed. "You'll be safer back here than in the front seat, okay?"

The heavy mesh screen separating the front and back seats made T.J. feel like he was putting a frightened animal into a cage. Noah was drenched and, as the next spear of lightning lit the night, T. J saw that he was shaking. T.J. wanted to dry him off but he had nothing to do it with. Rubbing the boy's matted hair, T.J. told him as calmly as he could manage that they were going to go get his mother. That was a ridiculous oversimplification but he couldn't think of anything else to say.

Rushing water battered the side of the cruiser as T.J. eased the heavy car, foot by foot, through the flooded driveway entrance. A bonfire of golden sparks engulfed a tangle of downed power wires blocking the roadway on the left, a spectacular display that made it clear which way Sonny had turned as he fled the townhouse development. T.J. accelerated onto Baltimore Avenue but slowed quickly when his rear tires hydroplaned wildly. "Hang on back there, Noah!" he yelled over his shoulder as the cruiser's headlights bored holes into the black night.

Doing his best to ignore the throbbing in his wounded ear, T.J. reached for the palm mike. "Sonny Masters is heading south on Baltimore Road, Chigger. He has Sandra Lucas with him. Her boy is safe with me."

"Description of the car?"

"I don't have one but I'm in pursuit."

"Be careful on those roads, T.J. There is flooding all over the county."

"Listen to me, Chigger, Frank Riley is dead. Sonny shot him."

"My God!"

"8657 Oak Ridge Court. It's the unit with a very large tree halfway through the roof. Get somebody out there right away."

"There's nobody to send, T.J. We just got a call that the WHCR radio tower was struck by lightning and fell across Magruder Street. Jenkins is heading over there right now." Chigger took a breath. "Problems are popping up faster than we can get to them. A couple of State

Troopers were on their way to help us out but got tied up when they spotted a jackknifed semi hanging off the Hamilton Street overpass out on 95."

"Is Sonny going to hurt my mother?"

T.J. barely heard the quiet words. He tried to find Noah in the rearview mirror but the inside of the car was too dark. "No. He is not." It was the only thing to say.

"Got to go, Chigger. I'll get back to you as soon as I can."

T.J. was pretty sure he had spotted taillights in the distance. He leaned forward, trying to focus through the overwhelmed windshield wipers, but did not see the two red dots again. Blinded by the rain, all T.J. could do was concentrate on what he could see of the yellow roadway lines and hope there was nothing in his way.

For seconds at a time, lightning transformed night into day, illuminating full-grown trees bent like saplings, their leaves filling the air like flocks of fleeing birds. A streetlight, ripped from its pole by the wind, bounced crazily onto the road and glanced loudly off the cruiser's front bumper. The sight of Mrs. Olsen's roadside mailbox, dazzling white in the unearthly light, signaled T.J. that he was no more than a hundred yards from the Cattail Creek bridge, a distance cut in half by the time the heavy car skidded to a stop. The roar of furious water underscored the heart-stopping scene frozen in his headlights: the bridge was gone! T.J. flipped on the cruiser's spotlight in time to catch sight of a huge tree, its branches flailing like the tentacles of a giant octopus, careening crazily downstream, followed seconds later by a white truss-like object. T.J. understood what had happened to the bridge the second he realized that the bobbing structure was a lifeguard stand. The old dam, a mile and a half upstream, had burst, unleashing the waters of a five-acre lake and sending it on a downstream rampage. As he started to back the cruiser away from the water's edge, the beam of its powerful spotlight caught a flotilla of wildly bouncing debris hung up on what appeared to be the roof of a car. The driving rain made it difficult to be sure, but T.J. could swear he had seen a frantically waving arm.

"Stay right there, Noah, don't move!"

The boy, wet and shivering, managed to nod his head.

T.J. did not want to leave him alone but had no choice. He slammed the door of the cruiser and ran to the end of the pavement. At his feet, the unrecognizable waters of Cattail Creek rampaged toward the Patuxent River, eight miles away, with a roar that could be heard above the howl of the storm. The submerged car, no more than thirty yards away, rocked violently in the wild current. There was no sign of the waving arm, but that didn't mean he was going to stand still and watch the car and the mountain of debris clinging to it break free and be swept away. Fighting through mud-covered underbrush, T.J. made his way upstream until a thick clump of willows, snapping madly in the unrelenting wind, kept him from going any farther. He dove into the water, swam hard toward the middle, and was immediately swept downstream.

CHAPTER THIRTY

The car had filled with water almost immediately after it plunged into the creek, leaving just enough of an air pocket beneath the roof for the two of them to breathe while they fought frantically to escape. Sandra's door, facing upstream into the raging current, might as well have been welded shut. On his side of the car Sonny groped desperately for the door handle. He found it, pushed down hard, and when he did, the door flew open with such force that he was almost swept downstream. He reached frantically for Sandra's arm, trying to drag her with him.

"Get out of the car!" Sonny screamed at Sandra as the water inside the car continued to rise. "Get out of the damn car!" He did not want her to drown. That had never been his plan. He grabbed her arm and pulled hard. Drowning would be much too easy for her. Countless times he had become delirious with pleasure imagining her pleading for mercy when she saw the knife in his hand, screaming that she would do anything he wanted her to do. If it was the last thing he did on this earth he was going to pull her sorry ass to shore and inflict every ounce of misery she had coming to her.

He yanked her arm once more but she fought back, gasping and coughing as the raging flood rocked the car like a toy. In a frenzy of anger and frustration, Sonny decided to do it to her while he could still breathe. He let go of the steering wheel to pull the knife from his jacket. The second he did, he was swept out of the car, twisting and tumbling beneath the black water, his clothes and skin ripped by sharp ends of the swirling, broken tree branches that filled the water. The overpowering force of the current slammed him hard against the rocky floor of the creek. Like an invisible monster, the angry flood grabbed him, shook him, and would not let go. For the first time in his life Sonny knew what it meant to panic. He hated the feeling. Sonny Masters might drown in some goddamned swollen creek, but he had never in his life experienced fear, and he was damned if he was going to start now. Fighting the powerful current with every ounce of remaining strength, unsure which way was up or which way was down, Sonny was about to lose consciousness when he slammed into a slimy wall of mud and grass and his head broke the surface. Gagging and coughing, vomiting muddy water, Sonny hung to clumps of wet grass, trying to catch his breath.

The fight with the unseen water monster had left him

sore and exhausted but, like every fight he had ever been in, he had won. As he pulled himself free of the raging creek he saw through the driving rain that the luckiest day of his life had delivered another present. High on a hill in front of him there were bright lights burning in the windows of a big house. Still on his hands and knees he turned, searching through the dark storm for the car. All he could see was the ghostly image of whitecaps crashing against a mass of bobbing debris. Sandra was dead; there was no doubt in his mind about that. He had been cheated out of the pleasure of taking a knife to her, but he couldn't help that. She had probably never made it out of the car and, even if she had, she would be a mile downstream by now, dead as a drowned cat. It wasn't the way he had planned it, but he was satisfied. He only hoped that she had used her last breath screaming for him to save her.

Sonny focused again on the warm, glowing windows at the top of the hill. He needed a car and he needed money and, if he stayed lucky, there would be a gun up there to replace the one he had lost in the water. Thunder rumbled like a formation of low-flying aircraft as he fought his way up the steep hill. "It's done," he told himself with a feeling as close to joy as he had ever experienced. He had shown the world one more time that nobody messed with Sonny Masters and got away with it. That was all that mattered. The only thing left was to get the hell out of here. Other than some vague notion of losing himself on the waterfront in Baltimore he hadn't thought much about how he was going to make that happen, but the way this day had gone so far, he had a feeling that the lights in those windows were pointing the way.

Chapter Thirty-one

Sandra was swept from the car seconds after Sonny, her flailing arms grasping blindly for anything that would keep her from being dragged into the violent abyss. As she fought to hold her breath, a mountain of tangled tree limbs collided with the violently rocking car, its largest branch spearing the vehicle's windshield and bringing the swirling mass to a stop. Sandra clung desperately to the quivering debris that ensnared her and screamed into the wind without hope.

T.J., hurtling head over heels downstream, slammed into the partially submerged car and was thrown over its roof into the same labyrinth of rubble that had trapped Sandra. The spike of a broken branch scraped his injured ear, igniting a spasm of pain so intense he almost vomited. Sandra, whom he had not seen, grabbed him around the neck, coughing words impossible to understand.

"Hold your breath!" he yelled above the thunderous roar of the surging water as he pulled her below the surface and dragged her free of the bobbing mass. Overwhelmed by the violence of the twisting current and gagging on muddy creek water, it was all T.J. could do to keep the panicked woman from being wrenched from his arms.

We're going to be fine," he had just finished shouting when, in a blinding flash of lightning, he saw, ten yards in front of them, the white frame of the lifeguard stand wedged in the remains of a huge tree that had been ripped from the creek bank. Holding the shaking woman with one arm, he grabbed the base of the truss-like structure and worked his way along its length until they reached water shallow enough for him to gain his footing and push Sandra ahead of him to the grassy bank. As he fought to catch his breath, golden lightning illuminated the long hill in front of them and silhouetted the familiar house at its crest, its many windows signaling through the storm like the lifesaving beams of a lighthouse.

"The woman who lives in that house told me this morning that any fool can operate a generator," T.J. laughed into Sandra's ear.

It was hard for him to believe that it had only been this morning when he dropped in on Verna Olsen to make sure she was okay. It seemed more like a week. "How does a hot cup of tea and a warm, dry house sound to you?" T.J. hollered above the wind as he pulled Sandra to her feet. The idea sounded good to him even if Verna insisted on lacing the tea with maple syrup. He might even give her a big hug and a kiss on the cheek when she opened her front door. Smiling at the thought, he took Sandra by the arm and urged her up the slippery hill. She took a few steps then pulled away and fell to the soggy grass. Pushing matted hair from her eyes, she held both hands close to her face and, to T.J.'s complete amazement, she said something about her fingernails being ruined and began to sob uncontrollably. "He was going to cut up my face! He said he had a knife and was going to cut up my face!" she wailed.

"Sonny Masters is gone, Mrs. Lucas; probably washed halfway down to the Patuxent River by now."

In truth, T.J. had not given a thought to Sonny Masters since his own miraculous encounter with Sandra Lucas in the middle of Cattail Creek. He glanced downhill toward the deafening sound of the angry creek, wondering for the first time if there was any chance that Sonny had somehow survived. If he were a gambling man, he told himself, he would bet his last dollar that days from now, maybe even weeks from now, some unlucky person would chance upon Sonny's bloated remains miles from where the bridge had washed out. That would be the time to worry about Sonny Masters, not now. "Come on," he said, pulling the shivering woman to her feet, "we need to make a little detour and get your boy. He's in my cruiser."

"Noah!" Oh my God!"

"He's okay. Come on, get up."

The wind fought their every step, at times so violently

that T.J. had to hold Sandra with both arms to keep her from being knocked off her feet. The spot on the steep road to the bridge where he had left his car was no more than fifty yards from Verna Olsen's driveway, but even to someone as strong as T.J., the struggle to reach it seemed to take forever. The reunion he witnessed when they finally reached Noah was totally unlike the joyous outpourings of emotion that had taken place the many times he had reunited lost children with their parents. There was little visible reaction by either mother or son. No hugs. No kisses. No crying. In the soft glow of the car light, Noah quietly asked if Sonny was gone and his mother replied that the bastard was gone forever. T.J. was pretty sure his own mother would have phrased her answer a little differently, but his mother had not been Sandra Lucas and—he was 100 percent sure on this point—his own mother would never have had anything to do with a man like Sonny Masters.

"Chigger, the Cattail Creek bridge is gone," T.J. announced into the radio when he was settled in the front seat.

"What do you mean gone, Chief?"

"Gone. All I can figure is that the old dam upstream washed out. Franny Kozar was supposed to send a public works crew down here to close the bridge but either he got tied up, or the barricades were swept away with everything else."

"Holy shit."

"Get somebody out here to set up flares on both sides

of the creek as soon as you can. Got that? And call Franny and tell him about the bridge."

Chigger Mason said he would do it and listened while T.J. gave him Mrs. Olsen's address and told him he would be there with Sandra Lucas and her boy.

"What about Sonny Masters?"

"I'm pretty sure he drowned in the creek. Did you find anybody to take care of Frank Riley's body?"

Before Chigger could reply, the overmatched antenna on the roof of the police station lost its battle with the storm and collapsed into the parking lot. T.J. didn't have time to find out if the outdated backup system was going to kick in. If it did, he might start believing in miracles.

Chapter Thirty-two

⎯⎯⎯⎯⎯ ∽∾∽ ⎯⎯⎯⎯⎯

"You poor, poor man!" had been Mrs. Olsen's reaction when she responded to Sonny Masters's furious pounding on her front door. He had dropped to his knees in exhaustion on her hall carpet, both of his shoes missing and as wet as she had ever seen a human being. She hurried to her linen closet to retrieve towels and a blanket to drape over his shoulders. To her great surprise, she found Sonny on his feet when she got back.

"Where's your husband!" he demanded. When she hesitated, confused and then alarmed by the man's angry tone, Sonny grabbed her roughly. "I said, where is your old man!"

Her instinct was to lie, and she did. "He'll be home any minute."

"You lying bitch!" Nobody is out in this storm." He slapped her hard. "Listen to me carefully and just maybe you'll live through this. I need some of your husband's clothes: some boots, a dry jacket, your car keys, and a gun."

"My husband is dead," she stammered.

Sonny shook her hard. "So he's dead! You old broads never throw away their clothes; show me where they are!"

Her face stinging from the handprint that had reddened her face, Mrs. Olsen put her hands on her hips and stared hard at Sonny. "Well, this old broad didn't. I gave them all to the Goodwill."

He slapped her so hard this time that her ears rang. Even as tears of anger and pain filled her eyes she became aware of the warm aroma of the banana nut bread she had put in the oven. She took a deep breath and informed Sonny that she had to take it out of the oven before it burned.

"Forget the fucking bread!" Sonny hissed. "Your husband had a gun, didn't he? A shotgun, a hunting rifle, I know he had something. You tell me you gave it to the Goodwill and I swear to God I'll beat you to death!" He twisted her arm until she could no longer stand the pain.

"It's out back in the shed."

"Where in the shed!"

"Hanging above the workbench."

She lied because she was afraid he was going to break her arm. Warren's shotgun was no longer hanging over his workbench. A year or two after he died she had donated it to the Hargrove Volunteer Fire Department for their Founders' Day Auction.

Sonny shoved her to the floor and ran out the back door. As she fell she hit her head hard on the sharp corner of the oak hallstand that had survived the long crossing from Denmark with her grandmother. Or was it her mother? Strangely, after all these years, she couldn't remember. Her thoughts seemed to be swimming in sleepy circles. Maybe T.J. could remember. He was a good boy. The lights in the house had come on just like he had said they would when she started the generator. She tried to call his name but her words were soundless and she was much too tired to try again. She had to get to the kitchen so she could turn off the oven, but she couldn't move. Tears filled her eyes. She had never burned banana nut bread, not even when she was a young bride.

Before Sonny had taken three steps from Mrs. Olsen's back porch, blinding lightning and earsplitting thunder sent shock waves through the night air, dropping him to the ground. Like a dazed boxer, he struggled to his feet and, in mud-caked socks and clothes so wet he had trouble moving, staggered through the avalanche of rain toward the work shed whose hiding place in the bending trees had been betrayed by the lightning. He needed that gun, and nothing was going to stop him from getting it. Maybe they would think he had drowned in that damn creek and maybe they wouldn't. All Sonny knew was that he had to get back on the road.

He pushed through the door of the shed. The rain drumming on its tin roof was deafening, but the sense of being sheltered from the pounding downpour was incredible. Involuntarily, he slumped to the floor. For the first time, he fixed his anger on the storm. Forgetting that its devastating sweep through Tennessee was the only reason he was a free man, he focused on the fact that the storm had robbed him of the chance to do the things to Sandra he had spent endless hours doing to her in his mind. As satisfying as his day of reckoning had been, it would have been even better to have had her for the last time, had her good with those long fingernails of hers slashing at him. Every time he had done it to her in his mind her desperate attempts to escape her fate had been the best part. He wanted her wild like an animal; just the thought of it had made his prison nights bearable. And then, when he was done, with his knees pinning her shoulders to the ground, he would have flashed the knife in front of her terrified eyes and started in on her beautiful face. Sandra on her back, begging for mercy: it would have been the most satisfying moment of his life. Golden lightning lit the small window above the workbench, jolting him back to reality. He smiled. After he was long gone, someone would find her in that creek, purpled and bloated, in a pile of trash and branches. That would be good enough. She had turned her back on Sonny Masters, and she had paid the price.

Sonny rose to his feet, the long, long day finally catching up with him. He had come too far and done too much to go back to prison. Someday he would wear fine clothes and expensive shoes again, drive fast cars and break cocky women like they were wild horses. All of that would be his once more, but right now he needed to get his hands on every dollar that old lady had stashed away inside her house; after that he needed to get the keys to her car and get moving. She would have to go; there were no two ways about that. He wasn't going to leave her behind to blab her fool head off. As soon as she found him some dry clothes and a pair of her dead husband's boots, he would do what he had to do and get the hell out of here. Sonny felt around in the darkness for the gun. When he found it he would be back in business.

The sound of the generator and the sight of warm yellow light in the windows facing Mrs. Verna Olsen's wind-swept front porch promised warmth and comfort and, knowing Mrs. Olsen the way T.J. did, a hot cup of tea and something wonderful from her oven. He rang the doorbell for the second time. Sandra, shivering as badly as Noah, put her arms around the boy. T.J. knew they would be out of their wet clothes and dried off in a few minutes. Verna would wrap the boy in a warm blanket and find something for Sandra to wear; it might not be the kind of thing she would pick out herself, but he was sure it would feel like heaven after what she had been through. T.J. peered in the window next to the front door. There was no one in the living room or in the part of the hallway that was visible. He knocked again, then tried opening the front door. It wasn't locked. The next time he was sitting in her kitchen he would remind her for the hundredth time to keep her doors locked, no matter how safe she felt in the house where she had lived for more than fifty years. She would smile and shake her head and ask him for the hundredth time who in the world did he think was going to bother an old woman like herself.

Inside, two things immediately caught his attention, the first one puzzling and the second one alarming. There was an enormous puddle of water on the floor right inside the door, and the air was filled with the smoky odor of burning food, experiences unknown in the Olsen house. Sandra noticed neither. What she noticed was Mrs. Olsen's overstuffed living room sofa where, without letting go of Noah, she collapsed.

Mrs. Olsen was dead. T.J. knew that from the second he saw her on the floor where she had fallen. He knelt beside her and, though he had seen so much death in so many forms, he thought the thoughts of a person to whom death is a stranger. He had just seen her this very morning; she had spoken to him the way she always did, like he was still a kid, trying to get him to drink maple-flavored hot tea and shooing him out of her house—this house—so she could get on with her day, storm or no storm. He touched her face and experienced a sense of devastation unknown to him since the day his mother died.

There was a time when he had known many prayers but, right now, the only one he could remember was the Our Father. The words didn't seem to fit, but he said them anyway. Crossing himself, he stood slowly and went into the kitchen to turn off the oven. As he came back into the front hall, shock and grief gave way to questions. Had she tripped? Did she have some kind of attack? He knelt beside her body again, noting the darkening blood that had matted the white hair at her left temple. There was not much blood, barely enough to form a small, perfectly round pool on the flowered carpet. He looked for, and found, a trace of the same dark blood on the sharp-cornered armrest of the ornate hallstand Verna had been so proud of. The policeman in him forced aside the grief-stricken friend who had known Verna Olsen since he was a boy. He understood the large puddle of water in the front hall and the significance of the wet trail marking a path to the back door.

The boy Noah, his hair matted and soaked clothes clinging to his thin body, wandered out of the living room and stared blankly at Mrs. Olsen's body.

"She's going to be okay," T.J. told him. "She fell and hit her head, but she is going to be okay." He led the boy back to the couch where his mother was staring up at the ceiling in a daze.

"I have to put the two of you in the cellar for a little while." Sandra Lucas was too exhausted to argue and almost too exhausted to stand.

"Sit right there on the stairs and don't make a sound until you hear my voice. Do you understand me?"

She nodded weakly. Noah twisted his head toward the hallway, trying to see if Mrs. Olsen had stood up yet.

"She's going to be all right," T.J. assured him again.

Noah stared up at him. "Does that hurt?" he asked, his young face reflecting concern as he studied T.J.'s blood-caked ear.

In fact, the ear that Sonny's bullet had ripped apart hurt like hell, a sharp stinging pain that competed for T.J.'s attention with the dull throb at the back of his head where Sonny had bashed him with the butt of his handgun.

"It's good. Now sit down next to your mother until I come back." He found the key on top of the doorframe where Mrs. Olsen always kept it and locked them in the cellar.

"Are you going to the doctor?" Noah called through the door.

"I will as soon as I can."

Outside, rain sheeted from the back porch roof, forming a virtual waterfall. Lightning strikes, so close together that they seemed like twin prongs of a giant fork, made direct hits on the Olsen property, one splitting an unseen tree with a loud crack and the other leaving a bathtub-size crater in the gravel driveway no more than fifty feet from the house. The white light of the double strike lingered long enough for T.J. to see that the door of the shed was open. He reached for his gun and found only an empty holster, a realization that distracted him from doing what he had to do as much as if he had noticed his shoe was untied.

CHAPTER THIRTY-THREE

Sonny was frantic. There was no weapon where the old lady had said it was. In his desperation to find it he had climbed on top of the workbench and run his bare hands along the wall, scraping his knuckles on hard, sharp objects he could not see in the dark. Like a blind man, he had then searched the entire pitch-black interior of the shed, cursing violently when he cracked his knee against the unyielding tow hitch on Mr. Olsen's ancient tractor. The string of obscene oaths had barely ended before he punctured his bare foot on the tines of an upturned rake and dropped to his knees in unbearable pain. "God damn it to hell!" he screamed in the darkness. "Somebody is going to get her head blown off when I get my hands on that gun!"

The brilliance of a lightning strike flared through the open door and the dusty window above the workbench. In the brief seconds of light Sonny saw nothing but junk and cobwebs. Another blinding flash lit the shed and still he saw no gun. With thunder rocking the shed and rain drumming like dropped gravel on its rusted metal roof, Sonny rose to his feet and stumbled across the bare earth floor toward the door, cursing a woman who was already dead.

Lightning fire was now virtually continuous, strike after strike bringing deafening explosions of thunder as Hurricane Chester swept eastward toward the sea. In the strobe-like flashes T.J. saw Sonny appear in the doorway of the shed and limp awkwardly out into the flooding yard where he began screaming incoherently as he started, head down, toward the house. The angry storm responded to his appearance by hurling a blinding column of lightning from its mantle of writhing clouds. The world seemed to explode. The ground shook with the force of an earthquake, slamming T.J. back against the wall of the house. In frozen frames of silver-white light, he saw Sonny suspended in the air, his arms and legs spread stiffly, his mouth open, and his hair and clothes on fire.

A sickening odor filled the darkness that followed, a stomach-turning stench that most people are blessed to never encounter. T.J. had not been so lucky. He had been a police officer for only two years the first time he was in the presence of burning flesh. In the wee hours of a December Sunday that he would never forget, the driver of a gasoline tanker had fallen asleep on the Interstate and swerved across the roadway, crushing a small sports car.

T.J. had been the first one to arrive at the scene and, all these years later, the only thing that made the memory of that horrible encounter bearable was the fact that he'd heard no screams. The college student at the wheel of the sports car had been killed instantly. That is what he had told her parents that day, and that is what he had told himself ever since.

The lightning strikes moving east with the storm continued to illuminate the night in an uncertain rhythm of light and darkness. Each golden flare revealed Sonny sprawled awkwardly on the rain-drenched ground. Struggling to his feet, T.J. eased down the porch steps and made his way slowly through the quagmire that was once Mrs. Olsen's well-tended yard. He watched for the slightest movement, ready for Sonny to spring to his feet, but it never happened. Sonny Masters lay on his back with one arm reaching stiffly toward the retreating black clouds. A tree branch, stripped of its leaves, lay across his chest. The blackened stub of a missing foot smoked like a charred log. His eyes and mouth were open wide, unfazed by the rain.

CHAPTER THIRTY-FOUR

Sonny Masters was not the last person killed by Hurricane Chester. The final recorded victim was seventy-nine-year-old Thomas Miller, who drowned in a pond on his farm near Seaford, Delaware, attempting to secure a line to the swim raft used by his grandchildren. By all accounts Mr. Miller was a good man who would be missed by everyone who knew him. "The best grandfather in the world," a twelve year-old granddaughter told a reporter for the *Seaford Weekly*. No one on earth would miss Sonny. The Tennessee Department of Corrections made it clear to the people in Maryland that they did not want his body shipped back to them. Media coverage of the devastating storm had pushed the story of his embarrassing escape from the headlines, and the TDOC intended to keep it that way.

As Sonny's unseeing eyes stared up at the final volleys of lightning, the dying storm reeled eastward toward the

Atlantic. The fury with which it had rained punches for seven hundred miles on both man and nature had taken its toll on Hurricane Chester, reducing it to a tropical storm, a reduction in rank that did not prevent it from ripping the tarpaulin from the infield at Oriole Park and flinging its shredded remains onto the roof of the B&O Warehouse high above the right field concourse. From there it crossed the northern Chesapeake, clawing desperately at the farm fields and raw subdivisions of northern Maryland, and mustered enough of a final punch to capsize a barge drifting free beneath the Delaware Memorial Bridge. This was to be Chester's final victory as, gasping for breath, it sought the warm waters of the open sea in a futile plea for rebirth.

Hurricanes are powerful and deadly in their prime, but they are not immortal. They are born of a combination of circumstances that shape them and send them on an angry path of destruction that does not end until they die. This one found no nurturing warmth in the green waters off the coast of the middle Atlantic the way it had in the sea west of Africa where it was born, or in the life-giving waters of the Caribbean where it had grown into an unstoppable force. Spiraling listlessly into the clearing skies above the eastern seaboard, the reeling giant died, its final breath unnoticed as giant tankers, bound for the oil terminal in Bayonne, New Jersey, plowed easily through the unnoticed remnants of its wrath.

In the United States alone, Hurricane Chester did more than 59 billion dollars' worth of damage and killed eighty-six people. Sonny Masters, the inmate Chester's destructive force released from prison, managed to kill four people before the storm caught up with him again and laid him in his grave, a final resting place more difficult to find than most. The refusal of the State of Tennessee to accept Sonny Masters's remains unrolled a ball of red tape that the State of Maryland finally tired of dealing with. His body, minus a foot that was never found, was cremated and interred as prescribed by law on the grounds of a state hospital outside of Baltimore. Birds carried off much of the seed scattered haphazardly over his grave by a maintenance crew in a hurry to break for lunch.

Men are shaped by kindness or cruelty and travel through life loving or hating, giving or taking. Sonny Masters lived like an angry animal, abusing and mistrusting all who came near. Only a brass number marked the small rectangle of earth where he was buried, and no one would ever say that there should have been more.

Chapter Thirty-five

All night long spinning ambulance lights lit the rain-slick roads leading to St. Joseph's Memorial Hospital, where every doctor and nurse on the roster had been called in to deal with victims of the hurricane. Corridors surrounding the emergency department overflowed with men, women, and children as the staff hurried among them seeking the most seriously injured and volunteers sought to comfort the others until there was a doctor available to see them. It was a scenario the staff at St. Joe's trained for regularly and one they hoped to never experience again.

At about four o'clock in the morning, a slot opened in one of the operating rooms and surgery was performed on T.J. Barnes's left ear. He welcomed the fitful sleep that overpowered him and awoke in need of pain medication that he refused to ask for. He slept again, and when he woke up this time the first hint of daylight had crept into his room. There was a bedpan within easy reach that he had no interest in using. With his ear on fire and dull pain radiating into his neck, he forced his unsteady legs across the floor to the bathroom. When he was done he leaned on the sink and stared into the mirror. The dressing on his ear looked like half of a softball, but no matter how hard he tried to turn his stiff neck, he could not see the wound on the back of his head where Sonny had hit him with the gun. A weak smile appeared in the mirror when it occurred to T.J. that he looked like a commercial for adhesive tape.

He made it back across the room at a pace that would have embarrassed a 110-year-old person and sat on the side of the bed, looking around for his clothes. The doctor who had operated on him, looking much too tired to be allowed back in surgery, came into the room, checked T.J.'s dressings, and took his pulse. "We took thirteen sutures in the back of your head while we were putting your ear back together. No extra charge," he said, doing his best to smile.

"Doctor humor?"

"I guess. It's been a long night." He explained that the operation had gone well but that the upper half of T.J.'s ear was missing. There were doctors at Johns Hopkins who specialized in ear reconstruction, he said, and he would give T.J. a name before he left the hospital.

Only seconds after the weary doctor left the room Noah appeared, the bathrobe he was wearing dragging along the floor behind him. He approached T.J. one careful step at a time, staring at the elaborately bandaged ear.

"My mother said Sonny shot your ear off."

"Not really. There's enough left to hear with. That's all that matters."

Noah seemed to think about that, involuntarily touching his own ear.

The nurse, who had twice instructed T.J. to stay in bed, swooped into the room carrying his neatly folded police uniform. She glared at him. "I had the people in housekeeping run these through the dryer, but don't you even think about putting them on. The doctor said you are to spend another night."

"Yes, ma'am."

"I'll yes ma'am you."

Before she spun to leave she shook a finger at Noah. "And you, young man, get back to your mother's room before she wakes up and has a fit."

Noah watched her leave.

"Did God kill Sonny?"

"What?"

"My mother said God killed Sonny."

"Your mother said that?"

The boy nodded.

T.J. was genuinely surprised. "Does your mother talk about God much?"

Noah shook his head. "We don't go to church."

T.J. didn't either. He respected people who did go, and sometimes wished he was as certain about the big question as they were. Long ago he had decided it was a waste of time to worry any more about it. There were things that made him believe there had to be a God, crazy things like dandelions growing in sidewalk cracks, reactions he would never confess to anyone. Whenever his thoughts started drifting in that direction he reminded himself about all the things he had seen in his life as a police officer, things like that young girl who had been crushed to death beneath a gasoline tanker. To this day he remembered her name, he remembered her age, and he remembered the fact that she had died on her birthday. If there was a God how could He, or She, or whatever God was supposed to be, allow things like that to happen? And how could any God allow a wonderful person like Verna Olsen to be killed by an animal like Sonny Masters? T.J. knew he wasn't smart enough to answer questions like that and told himself once again that it wasn't worth worrying about.

"Sonny got struck by lightning," he told Noah honestly.

"My mother said that's how God killed him."

T.J. stood up, paused a second to let the dizziness calm, and walked slowly to where Nurse Ratched had left his clothes. "I wish God had left that job to me."

He should have never said something like that to a child. He looked at Noah, wishing he could take it back, but of course he couldn't. Noah stared back at him thoughtfully then nodded like he understood—and for all T.J. knew, he did.

Nurse Ratched appeared out of nowhere and snatched the still-warm uniform from T.J. "I changed my mind. You will get this back when the doctor says you are ready to leave this hospital and not one minute sooner!"

Noah watched her leave then looked back at T.J.

"Will you marry my mother?"

T.J. struggled to speak. "What?"

"Then you will be my father."

T.J. had the crazy thought that he was hallucinating, either from the anesthesia or from having his head split open. He closed his eyes for a few seconds and opened them again. Noah had moved a few steps closer to the bed.

"Your mother and I don't know each other very well. I think we are very different kinds of people." T.J. was doing his best to say the right thing to a boy who was obviously even lonelier than he had imagined.

"She is pretty."

"I know, but . . ." T.J. had no idea what to say.

Noah twisted the bathrobe's belt until it was a tangle of terry cloth. "Then, can we be friends?"

Sandra Lucas stood in the doorway. She looked terrible. The entire left side of her face was purple and swollen and her left eye was almost closed. In the darkness and rain, even in the warm glow of Mrs. Olsen's house, T.J. had failed to notice how badly Sonny had hurt her.

"Noah, I have been looking all over for you," she scolded halfheartedly. "And you in your bare feet." She reached her hand toward him. "Let's get back to the room before I fall down."

"Noah," T.J. called after them. The boy turned.

"We *are* friends."

Noah said something to his mother as they walked down the hallway, but T.J. could not hear what it was.

"Mrs. Hogan tells me she can't get you to stay in bed."

T.J. turned from the window where he had been counting the downed light poles in the parking lot below. He couldn't read the nametag of the nurse standing in the doorway, but he didn't have to.

"She said you are the most hardheaded patient she's ever had to deal with."

"Who said that?" T.J. managed to ask.

"Mrs. Hogan, your nurse."

"Oh, you mean Nurse Ratched."

"That's not very nice, T.J. She's a very good nurse and, like the rest of us, she's had a very long night." Mary Beth Banakowski stood with her hands on her hips, struggling to keep a smile hidden behind the mask of a stern head nurse. "Come on, T.J., get back in bed."

He glanced over at the hospital bed but didn't move. The last time they had spoken—really spoken—they had been sitting in his car on a cold Christmas Eve right after he first joined the police force. He had known what she was hoping for that Christmas. He had even bought the ring.

"It sounds like you had quite a night," she said into the heavy silence that had filled the space between them.

"I'm sure you did too. Everyone did."

"At least nobody shot me in the ear."

All T.J. could think to say was, "It must have been your lucky night."

They both laughed nervously then stood staring at each other until a woman's efficient voice announced over the speaker system that Mrs. Banakowski was needed at the surgical nursing station.

"Got to go," she said quietly.

"Mary Beth, I'm sorry," he said.

She looked at him for a long time. "You say that like it was just last night."

CHAPTER THIRTY-SIX

While leaving a meeting with the heads of various county departments involved in the ongoing cleanup efforts, T.J. took a call from his secretary, Helen Burgess.

"A Mrs. Banakowski called from St. Joe's hospital."

T.J. stopped halfway through the front door of the county office building. "And?"

"Forgive my curiosity, but did you leave the hospital in your underwear?"

"No. I had Jenkins stop by my house and bring me a clean uniform. They weren't going to let me leave."

"So I gathered. I felt like a mother receiving a phone call from the school principal about a misbehaving child. Mrs. Banakowski said your uniform and your medical discharge papers are waiting for you in her office."

T.J. smiled as he pushed through the door into the most beautiful late-summer day he had ever seen. There was nothing he would rather do than slip over to the

hospital right then and there, but he was on his way to
deal with an agitated vice president at BGE, a man who
saw no reason why every road in the county could not be
closed while his crews repaired downed power lines and
light poles. After getting that little matter straightened
out, everything else was going to take a back seat while
he paid a visit to St. Joe's and took his medicine.

Because the Hargrove county council and the acting
county executive could not agree where the funds were
going to come from, reconstruction of the old dam on
Cattail Creek remained in limbo, meaning that the public
swimming hole that had been an institution for generations might well become a memory. On the other hand,
because they were afraid of angering the many voters
who had to cross the creek daily, a new bridge at the
Baltimore Road crossing was already in the design stage.
Week after week, proposals for funding its construction
remained the hottest topic on the agenda. At one meeting,
while T.J. Barnes waited restlessly to address the council about the needs of his police department, a woman
near the front of the room waved her hand for attention.
She had done the same thing a number of times during
the meeting and been ignored. This time several of the
council members glared at her before continuing debate
on their latest idea for funding the new bridge: charging
a toll.

"A toll bridge on a two-lane road used by commuters and school busses? You must be a bunch of imbeciles!" shouted the hand-waving woman. "Why don't you raise the money for the bridge by eliminating your salaries!" she continued, jumping to her feet. "All of you get free cars, free gasoline at the county garage, and God knows what else! It's a hell of a lot more than you deserve!"

All five council members turned white. One or two cleared their throats, and one pretended to study the ceiling. The acting county executive, Crunch Babcock, the second-generation owner of Babcock's Pest Control, pounded his gavel. "Madam," Crunch proclaimed in the same squeaky voice T.J. remembered from high school, "I have not opened this meeting to public discussion!"

"Well, you should!"

Things in Hargrove County were returning to normal.

On the Maryland coast, where families had gradually returned to the beaches, parents looked up from their paperbacks or interrupted conversations to watch children playing at the edge of the surf. The memory of the storm had healed like a wound and life had moved on. Hassles with insurance companies seemed to be never-ending but, for the most part, roofs had been repaired and downed trees cut up and hauled away.

Twelve hundred miles away, a Caribbean fishing village held funeral services for the husbands, sons, and brothers whose bodies would never be found. Fr. Martin led a procession of altar boys from his church on the cobblestone square down to the edge of the water where the government dock had been located. Those who could bear to do so stared at the endless horizon. Children fidgeted nervously, and their mothers cried quietly as the rosary was said and flowers were scattered on the quiet water. Fr. Martin raised his hand to bless the sea then, one at a time, recited from memory the names of those the storm had taken. The old priest had done this before and was certain that, if he lived long enough, he would do it again. He had seen enough in his long life to know that these young altar boys, earnestly shielding the fragile flames on their candles from the gentle breeze, would someday take to the sea themselves and chase the fish that would feed their families and provide a few dollars to spend on rum at the Limon Cielo. Their fathers had done it and their uncles and brothers had done it and, despite his fervent prayers, these boys would do it also. It was the way of life in the small world they knew and, too often, it was the way their uncomplicated lives would end.

CHAPTER THIRTY-SEVEN

T.J. found Verna Olsen's worn address book in a kitchen drawer. In it there was a phone number for a Marva Krause in Pekin, Illinois. He thought he remembered, correctly as it turned out, that Marva Krause had been Verna's sister, the one she called the Roller Derby Queen. His experience had been that informing someone in person about the death of a family member was extremely difficult but that doing it over the telephone was even worse. Over the years he'd had to do it by phone two other times, and the call he made to Marva Krause made him hope to hell he never had to do it again.

"What? What's that?"

"Could you please turn down your television, ma'am."

"This ain't no library; it's a bar. Got a bunch of customers watching NASCAR on my new flat screen."

T.J. had no choice but to yell what he had to say into the phone.

"Verna, what about her?"

The entire phone call, placed the day T.J. left the hospital, had gone that way and, despite having his secretary, Helen, call again after Verna's arrangements were complete, Mrs. Krause did not show up for the funeral. She sent no note or flowers, but about a month later she sent her son, one Herman Krause, to check out the house she was in line to inherit. T.J. met him when a neighbor called to report that someone was sitting on Verna's front porch, smoking a cigarette.

"You drove all this way?" T.J. asked him, noting the Illinois plates on the beat-up Jeep in the driveway.

"You got it," the unshaven man wearing a faded Pink Floyd tee shirt answered, heaving his scuffed work boots onto the railing. He took a final drag on his cigarette and flipped it into the boxwoods that lined the porch. "What the fuck happened to that bridge?" he asked, nodding down the hill toward Cattail Creek.

Over the years, T.J. had gotten better about making quick judgments. Better, but not perfect. He struggled to conceal the fact that he had no use for the man who was sitting on Verna's front porch like he owned the place.

"Hurricane destroyed the dam a couple of miles upstream."

Herman Krause spit over the rail. "Must have been a pretty shitty dam."

T.J. asked the man for his driver's license.

"I'm a Krause. This is my mama's house, least way it's going to be when the dust settles. She told me that."

T.J. asked him again for his driver's license and, after satisfying himself that the man was indeed Mrs. Krause's son, he reluctantly unlocked the front door with the key that had been his since he was a teenager.

"How much you think this old place is worth?" Herman Krause asked after taking a quick look around.

T.J. shrugged his shoulders. "Didn't see you or your mother at Verna's funeral."

"So."

"Seems like it would have been the right thing to do. Especially since you had the time to drive all the way down here to check out her house."

"My mama's got a bar to run."

T.J. had a hard time believing that Verna Olsen was related to people like these. He wondered why she hadn't left the house to her church or to some charity. As he watched Herman Krause light another cigarette and drop the match on the neatly painted porch, it occurred to him that she may have intended to do just that but never gotten around to it. Verna had no idea she was going to die in the storm; the only thing on her agenda that day was baking banana nut bread, something he had trouble picturing her Roller Derby sister doing.

When Herman Krause put his hand out for the key to the house, T.J. told him he would have to wait until his mother legally took possession of the property.

Herman looked hard at T.J. "My mother is not going to be happy about this."

Since T.J. could not think of a way to say *tough shit* politely, he said nothing at all.

From the back of his Jeep Herman Krause removed a "House For Sale" sign that looked like it came off the shelf of a hardware store. After scrawling a phone number on it with a Magic Marker, he pounded the sign into the ground in the middle of the Olsens' front yard and left without saying another word. For his part, T.J. did not point out to Herman Krause that he had neglected to include an area code with the phone number. Two months later the grass in a two-foot radius around the sign was knee-high. That was as close to the sign as T.J. could get when he used Warren's old tractor to mow the acre of property surrounding the empty house.

One Sunday morning, after mowing the long slope from the house to the creek, T.J. slipped Warren's old tractor into neutral and unscrewed the cap of a water bottle. The creek at the bottom of the hill flowed almost imperceptibly, a moving mirror reflecting sky and willows. Two boys with fishing poles sat atop one of the concrete buttresses from which the Cattail Creek Bridge had been wrenched. The county had erected barricades and "No Trespassing" signs on both sides of the creek, but T.J. wasn't going to do anything. He couldn't think of a better way for two boys to spend such a beautiful morning.

Reconstruction of the bridge was scheduled to begin by the end of the month. Facing an increasingly vocal revolt by frustrated commuters, the council had stopped arguing long enough to fund the project. Not only that, but in a move that had surprised T.J. and made him wonder if it was actually possible that they had feelings like normal human beings, the council members had voted to name the reconstructed bridge for Fat Frank: The Francis G. Riley Memorial Bridge, a name worthy of a structure mighty enough to span the Chesapeake Bay. Nobody was ever going to call it that—it would always be the Cattail Creek bridge—but though Fat Frank had never been one of his favorite people, he had witnessed the terrible way the man had died and had no problem with the decision. T.J. had attended the late county executive's funeral, an overdone affair with flowery testimonials that no one meant and at which only one person— Fat Frank's wife, Francine—cried. It was obvious that someone had loved the man, someone who counted, and maybe that was all it took to make a person's life work. T.J. had stopped Mrs. Riley after the service and told her he was sorry for her loss. He told her that her husband had been a good man. Lies weren't always bad. Nobody could have convinced him of that when he was a young man, but he believed it now.

Verna Olsen had been the one who told him that telling a lie wasn't always a bad thing. She told him that the lines of behavior softened as a person got older. Sitting in that big old kitchen with the snake plants on the windowsill, having maple syrup–laced tea with her because she never drank coffee, she had made that statement out of the blue. "The lines blur and you find that isn't so bad. All those hard little boxes into which we cram the prejudices and beliefs of a lifetime start to come apart and everything, all the different colors and shapes and all the *shall-nots* and *thou-shalts*, spill into one big pile and we don't know how to sort them out again because we are no longer sure we had them in the right order in the first place." She had stared out her kitchen window, at the old shed where her husband Warren had spent his happiest hours and at the tall trees separating her green yard from the summer sky. After being quiet for a long time, she had laughed. "Don't mind me, T.J., I'm getting old."

Taking a long pull from the water bottle, T.J. studied the big house at the top of the hill. While the first-floor windows slept in the deep shadow cast by the wide porch, the bedroom windows above it reflected the brilliance of the noonday sun, golden rectangles that he imagined could be seen for miles. It wasn't until he restarted the tractor and began cutting the grass along the edge of the creek that T.J. was struck by the terrible thought that would live with him for the rest of his life: Verna Olsen would still be alive if it were not for him.

He disengaged the cutting disc, wiped his brow with the back of his hand, and looked up at the house again. Somewhere not far from where he was sitting, Sonny Masters had crawled out of the creek that night like a half-drowned animal. Desperate and disoriented, he would have had no idea which way to turn until, through the blinding rain, the lighted windows at the top of the hill summoned him like outstretched arms. Verna Olsen had died because of those lights. If he had not badgered her into installing a generator, if he had not insisted that she learn how to use it, she would still be up there at the top of the hill, fussing with her flower boxes or, on a warm morning like this, sitting in the cool shade of her porch, reading the paper. There would come a time when T.J. would no longer notice his shattered ear, but there would never be a time when he would forget why Verna had died. He turned in the tractor seat and studied the two boys fishing from what was left of the Cattail Creek Bridge and came as close to praying as he ever did. If there is a heaven, his silent words implored, may it be as perfect as this beautiful morning.

CHAPTER THIRTY-EIGHT

—⚬⚬⚬—

That fall, T.J. ran into Sandra Lucas and her boy coming out of the new Cracker Barrel on Baltimore Road. It would have been an exaggeration to say his relationship with the woman had reached the point where her face lit up when she ran into him, but she did say *hello* and then *fine* when he asked her how she was doing. Her son Noah was wearing shoulder pads, a grass-stained jersey, and football pants, a development that surprised T.J. but made him happy.

"Did your team win?" T.J. asked.

Noah shook his head. "I dropped a pass."

It was obvious to T.J., who had played more football than any sane person ever should, that Noah's shoulder pads were on backwards, a detail he was reluctant to point out to Sandra, who probably knew as much about football as he knew about fingernail polish.

"We're going to practice catching in the backyard

when we get home," Sandra Lucas interjected, dramatically transforming T.J.'s opinion of her.

He would have loved to toss a football with Noah, showing him how to catch the ball not with his body but with his hands, the way all the good receivers he had played with in college caught passes. It dawned on him that there was a lot he could teach Noah about football, starting with how to put his pads on correctly. As he was about to open his mouth on the subject it also dawned on him that he might be butting into a situation that was none of his business.

Slipping back into his police cruiser, T.J. remembered that the thirty-year reunion of the last Maryland team he had played for—a great bunch of guys who had beaten a very good Florida team in the Gator Bowl his senior year—was coming up. He had never been to one of his football reunions, but because his old teammate Duke Cumberland wouldn't stop bugging him about it, he was leaning toward going to this one. He wondered if Sandra Lucas would let him take Noah down to College Park and watch the Terps play North Carolina that day. Even if she did, it was entirely possible that the boy, as shy as he seemed to be, would have no interest in going. T.J. watched Noah and his mother drive out of the parking lot ahead of him. What a special thing it would be, he decided as he pulled out onto the road behind them, if when he and Duke and all the other old farts were introduced, he could walk out onto the field with a boy like Noah at his side. T.J. wasn't used to having thoughts like that, but he liked the way it felt. Maybe doing it would create a good memory for Noah to stack next to all the rough ones he had experienced in his young life.

All he could do was ask.

ABOUT THE AUTHOR

Thomas Clark was born in Washington, D.C., in 1941 and educated at Gonzaga College High School and at the Catholic University of America. He spent his working career practicing architecture before retiring to devote more time to writing. He lives in West River, Maryland, with his wife, Roz, and can be contacted at heyutom@comcast.net.

Made in the USA
Middletown, DE
27 April 2021

38127979R00149